don't

say

a word

JENNIFER
REBECCA

don't say a word

Captain Liam Goodnite has everything he's ever wanted right at the tip of his fingers: an enviable career, a beautiful girlfriend, and a brand-new baby daughter.

So why can't he let the ghosts of the past rest? Lee spends his nights plagued by memories, and when members of the old team succumb one by one to their demons, Lee can't help but wonder if he should talk about it.

But then he remembers the eternal vow the band of brothers spoke that long-ago night.

No matter what you do, *don't say a word.*

author's note

Hello lovely friends,

I know you have been waiting for Lee's final book and the hope he will get his happily ever after, and he will, but as always with my heroes, it's not an easy road for them to travel. I wanted to give you a heads up that Don't Say a Word addresses PTSD, veteran suicide, and various forms of mental illness. If this is not for you, I understand completely. If you want to skip ahead and read the conclusion, do it! If you can't do it at all, I want you to know that's totally cool too.

My husband, Sean, and I both come from families with a long-standing military history, Sean himself having served in the United States Navy Submarine Service. And with that, we have seen too many friends, good men and women, struggle with demons.

Every day, twenty-two veterans and one active duty service member end their lives due to PTSD. Twenty-two. I'll let that sink in. That's roughly one hundred sixty-one per week, six hundred ninety per month, or eight thousand three hundred ninety-five every year.

One is too many.

If you struggle with PTSD, depression, or anxiety, you

are not alone. I know, because for two years, I struggled with Postpartum Depression (PPD) and whether or not I had value. I struggle with anxiety every day. And every day, my family walks that journey with me. So from the trenches, I want to tell you that you matter; your loved one matters.

If you or someone you know is contemplating suicide, please contact the National Suicide Prevention Center: 1-800-273-8255

Here are several organizations who specialize in veterans:
Valhalla Project
Stop 22
Got your 6

Love always,
Jennifer (& Sean too)

For anyone who struggles with anxiety or depression,
you are not alone.
If you find yourself down a dark road,
don't be afraid to ask for a flashlight.
#IamYOU

And also for Sean,
who loves me anyways,
and Always.
Even more when I don't deserve it.

Even if we're breaking down, we can find a way to break through

Even if we can't find heaven, I'll walk through hell with you

Love, you're not alone, 'cause I'm gonna stand by you

Even if we can't find heaven, I'm gonna stand by you

Even if we can't find heaven, I'll walk through hell with you

Love, you're not alone, 'cause I'm gonna stand by you

-Rachel Platten

don't
say
a word

prologue

all my fault

I t's all my fault.

The smell of sulfur fills my nostrils, and smoke sears my lungs. The heavy weight of the rifle in my hands is like second nature to me. I could carry it in my sleep. During training, I probably did.

But it's the eyes that chill me to the bone in the middle of this hot desert.

I don't know how the intel had gone so bad. I know it happens, but not like this. One minute, the mission was going to plan, and the next, the world exploded. Spurts of gunfire can be heard all around me, but it's the screams that ring in my ears.

"Fuck, fuck, fuck!" I hear Adams scream through the comm in my ear. "They're dead. They're all dead."

And he's right. They're all dead. Every last one of

them. I was helpless to prevent this, but still, I feel like I should have. It's as bad as if their blood was directly on my hands.

The smoke burns my throat as I turn to the left and see Emma's blonde-and-pink hair, her blue eyes open and watching me, her beautiful body mutilated, because I was in her life.

"No!" I shout.

But the eyes of the dead scream that this is all my fault.

"It's all my fault," I mumble. My throat is raw from the smoke inhalation, and the screams echo in my ears, but still, I know that's not right, right?

"That's right," a familiar voice coos. "It's all your fault."

"My fault."

"Yes, Captain Goodnite. It's your fault, and now you have to pay."

"It was you," I gasp as I fade in and out of consciousness while the noose tightens around my neck when it's pulled tight. "It was all you."

"Yes." They laugh. "It was all me."

"Not my fault."

"Oh no, it's very much your fault, and now you're going to die."

And then she raises my hand holding my gun to

my head. Where did that come from? I locked it away, didn't I? *I can't remember… I can't remember….* The memories—that's all I remember.

I wasn't ready to go, but I guess it's like they say, *"Life's a bitch, and then you die."*

My name is Captain Liam Goodnite with the George Washington Township Police Department, and it looks like I'm about to die. Every story has an ending, and this one's gonna sting.

one

livin' the dream

I snap the file folder closed on my desk. Jones and I were able to close another case, and I spent the last hour writing up the report, because if I hadn't, it would have sat on Jones's desk until the end of time.

Was I ever this bad about paperwork when I was a detective?

The thing is, I don't think I was. When I got out of the Navy and got hired on at the police department, I dove into work like it was a lifeline, because that's exactly what it was. I was drowning, and work was the only thing to give me something else to focus on other than the demons that lived inside me.

Well, that and a night in bed with a beautiful woman, but that was just a Band-Aid on a gunshot wound.

A quick fuck might have felt good in the moment,

but it left me feeling emptier than I had before.

And then I made a fatal mistake.

I knew Anna had her own demons; I could see them dancing in her ice-blue eyes. I knew she wanted more than one night, and I knew without a doubt that I couldn't give it to her. But I fucked her anyway. I had become sloppy in my need to quiet the voices in my head, and while my sister's life was spinning out of control, I slept with not one coworker, but two.

Then I fell in love with the second one.

And the first woman died.

It's been a long two years. Ones I never thought would see me living with the woman who stole my heart and our beautiful daughter. And like those stupid T-shirts you can buy in the shops at an airport terminal say, life is good.

But there's still something missing.

I'm restless. I'm anxious. And there is a voice deep inside me that whispers that I don't deserve any of this: the beautiful girlfriend I've just asked to marry me, the daughter that is a miracle in so many ways—the biggest of which is all she and her mother have already survived—and a happy life, because of what we did— or didn't do, really—in the desert.

I spy the empty coffee mug on my desk and wonder if I should grab another cup. Sometimes, I feel like I should just get an IV tap in my arm to fuel the caffeine into my body at all hours. Actually, I wonder if that's something my soon-to-be bride could do. On second thought, scratch that. That is probably wildly inappropriate and wholly unacceptable... or illegal.

There's a knock at my office door.

"Enter," I call out.

I'm never really sure what the day will bring here. This is a small department in a tiny, little township in northern New Jersey. In theory, nothing ever happens here, but that's not true at all. This town is filled with dangerous secrets and malice, and it's my job to keep the demons at bay.

The doorknob turns, the heavy panel swings open, and my breath catches in my lungs as my heart beats faster in my chest. I breathe in slowly and hold it, and then I take in another breath without letting it go. I suck in one more and hold it all, feeling the burn in my lungs, and then I slowly let it all out like a balloon with a pin leak. It does little to quell my anxiety, but at this point, I'll take anything. Today has been a good day, and yet I'm still struggling. Emma and the baby are home safe, and their attackers are dead. I shouldn't worry... *and yet I still do*.

I hate that I can't control this. I control everything about my life. I don't like wild and crazy; my sister's YOLO attitude has added more gray hairs to my head than anything else. And I don't just like order and precision—I crave it. And I don't have it.

Wes pokes his head in the opening of the door before stepping inside.

"Hey, man," he greets me. "How's it going?"

"Living the dream," I say, smiling a smile I don't completely feel. *What is wrong with me?* I am living the dream... *my dream.* I finally have Emma in my life and our gorgeous daughter, Hope. My career is everything I've worked for, and I know that one day I will be Chief of Police.

But I can't help feeling like it's all one big fucking lie.

Am I living a lie?

I watch as Wes looks me over and takes my measure. I wonder what he sees when he looks at me. Does he see on my skin the doubt and darkness that lives inside me? Some days it feels like it's gone forever, and other days, like today, it feels like a tattoo I wear across my skin—permanent and ugly for all to see.

"So Emma's back at work?" he asks.

"Yeah," I answer with a sigh as I push a hand through my hair. I'm not ready for her to be back at work, but at the same time, I did not like having her away from me all day. I need to know she and Hope are safe, because it's my job to keep them that way, and I've already failed once.

"You don't sound so sure," Wes says as he leans against my office door.

"It's complicated."

"I feel that," he replies. "I'm pretty fucking glad Claire decided to take an extended maternity leave to be with the twins. Overjoyed."

"Yeah." I can't help the smile that pulls my lips at the thought of my kid sister, a girl who grew up to be a tough-as-nails detective and now a loving mother. "I can't lie. I like seeing my sister happy."

"Me too," he agrees. "I'd die to keep her that way, but she's going to kill me first."

"Uh oh." I laugh, grasping at the distraction of how I'm a mess and my sister finally has it all together. "What did you do now?"

"It's more like what I'm refusing to do," he says cryptically.

"And that is?" I can't help but get my back up a bit. Wes has been my best friend our entire lives, but if he hurts my sister, I'll kill him, and he knows it. Fortunately, he also knows that if he hurts her, she'll probably kill him before I have a chance to.

"She's already talking about more babies."

"It's been six weeks!" I shout. "Is she crazy?"

"I think you know the answer to that," he replies as he rolls his eyes.

"Watch your words when you're talking about my sister, buddy," I warn.

"Tell me I'm wrong," he prompts as he stares me down, and I laugh.

"You're not, but brotherly habits are hell to break."

"I bet," he says. "She scared the hell out of me. I thought I was going to lose her. I thought I was going to lose all of them."

"I know."

"I know you know, brother," Wes says. He looks away, lost in his own dark memories for a second before he turns back to me. "What a club we belong to, huh?"

"It's a shitty club." And it's true. Who wants to be the guy whose wife almost died in childbirth? That's not supposed to happen anymore. Women aren't dropping babies in wheat fields only to pick up a plow an hour later. My sister was supposed to safely deliver her twins. My woman was supposed to be safe in my home with almost two months left of her pregnancy before she delivered. She wanted to try a natural birth. She wanted to have more children. She didn't get either of those, and I didn't stop it.

The guilt I carry is immense.

"That it is," he agrees. "So… Emma's good?"

"Yeah," I reply. "She's happy to be back, and I'll admit I like knowing she's close."

"She's okay away from Hope?"

"She is, because Hope is with my mom during the day," I tell him. "And Dad and Seth are spoiling her rotten."

"I bet." He laughs.

"And Brooklyn is getting a fair idea that she's not ready for a baby anytime soon."

"Thank God," Wes says. "I'd hate to have to commit murder."

"Same." I chuckle. We didn't grow up with our sister, Bonnie, but now that she's gone, her kids are finally part of the family. I hate that we didn't get to know her, but I love that they are finally where they belong, even though that victory is bittersweet. But still, Wes and I did a damn good job scaring off Brooke's last boyfriend. I like to think it's our duty as her uncles, since her brother, Eric, is off in the Army.

"God, that kid was a pussy," he says.

"Thank fuck he's gone."

"One day," he adds quietly, "someone is going to love her like she deserves, and we're going to have to let her go."

"As long as it's not today," I hedge boldly. We both know it's a lie.

"It's going to happen someday," he warns.

"I know." I sigh. "It's weird. I haven't known Brooke her whole life, but still I know that none of the knuckleheads here deserve her."

"Truth."

"Just wait until Hope dates."

"Never happening," I tell him.

"It will."

"Probably right after Anna Faith gets married."

"I'll kill you."

"I'm not afraid of you." I laugh.

"Okay, I'll have Claire kick your ass at family dinner tonight."

"Fuck!"

"You forgot, didn't you?" He smirks.

"No!" I lie. "Yes."

"Come on, let's go get your girl and head to dinner."

"Shit," I mutter as I lock up my desk and shut down my computer.

I close the file I had open on my desk and stuff it into the rack on the top of my desk, when the door to my office opens and Emma strolls in. She takes one look at me and stops just this side of the door with her hand on her hip that's cocked out to the side. There's a little look of exasperation on her face mixed with a bit of irritation, and it's sexy as hell. I hate that we have to go to a family dinner right now, when I'd rather take her home and make love to her instead.

But there's always later.

"You forgot about family dinner, didn't you?" she asks me.

Wes chuckles from his seat in front of my desk.

"Yes," I answer reluctantly.

"Well, come on then," she says with a mischievous smile dancing around her pink lips.

I push up from my chair and walk around my desk, pulling her into my arms. I press my mouth to hers quickly and then let her go.

"Shall we?" I ask as I grab my leather jacket from the hook by the door.

"I'll meet you guys there," Wes says as I pull open the door for Emma and follow them through.

"Sounds good."

I lead Emma through the hallway outside my office and through the back of the station. She already had her jacket and her bag in her arms and was changed out of her scrubs and into jeans and a pretty blue blouse my mom had bought her on a shopping trip, so I knew she was ready to go. I push open the glass door at the rear of the station, and we step out into the still warm evening. It won't be long before the air turns cold, but still, I'll take an Indian summer when I can.

I pull my keys from my front pocket and hit the button on the key fob. The locks beep open, and I pull open the passenger door for Emma and offer her a hand as she climbs up into the SUV.

"Thanks," she says sweetly as she plants her ass in the seat with a soft smile on her face.

"Of course."

"I love you, Lee."

"I love you," I reply with a smile just before I shut the door and make my way around the hood of the car to climb in the driver seat. I hit the ignition and turn to Emma. "Let's go get our girl."

And then I make my way through town toward my childhood home.

I pull up to the curb out front, and Wes parks behind me. The long driveway is already full of cars that I know belong to Brooklyn and her friends. Sometimes, it's absolutely fucking surreal to see the next generation gathered in this house over algebra homework and talk of homecoming dates. My parents absolutely love it.

"Uncle Lee!" Seth shouts as he runs toward me the minute I walk through the door.

"Seth!" I call out as I swoop him up into my arms and hang him upside down over my shoulder, making him giggle. "What's up, my man?"

"I'm so high up!" he shouts. "You're so tall."

I laugh at his seven-year-old antics. "I am."

"But not as tall as Uncle Wes."

"That's because Uncle Wes is really an ogre," I tell him conspiratorial.

"Like Shrek?" Seth asks.

"Yes," I answer excitedly. "Just like Shrek."

"That's just silly." He laughs.

"It is," I agree as I set him back on his feet. "Where's Grandma?"

"Right here, son," my mom says, stepping out of the kitchen as she wipes her hands on a dish towel. "It's good to see all my babies together. I love you."

"I love you too, Mama."

"Come here, my other daughter," she tells Emma

before pulling her into her arms. This is something Mom had started calling Emma when she would come around to hang with Claire much like Brooke is with her friends now.

"Hi, Mama."

"Now, where's my baby?" I ask.

"Good luck trying to pry her from your father's arms," Mom says, making me laugh.

"He can't hold all three babies at once," I remind her. "So he'll have to let me have mine back."

"We'll see," she says cryptically, making Emma chuckle.

I hear my dad's booming laugh followed by a baby squeal and follow them into the family room. I have no trouble finding my dad. He's in the center of the room with the sofas pushed back to make the open floor space bigger, and spread in the middle of the carpet is a big quilt with three babies sprawled on it while my dad shakes rattles and pushes buttons on toys that light up and play music. One in particular would make my eye twitch if my beautiful baby girl didn't love it so much.

"There are my boys!" Dad says happily when he sees Lee and me. "Hey, Emma."

"Hi, Dad," she says with a soft smile on her face just for my old man.

Where she had been apprehensive around my family before, now Emma is a part of the whole the way she never let herself be before. My family immediately brought her into the fold, making it clear that she was a Goodnite, and it was always going to be that way moving forward. And I fucking love it.

But Dad and Emma have a unique relationship. Having no father of her own, Emma had never been doted on by an adoring father. That ended when he became her number-one champion. If we fight, Dad takes her side, claiming that even if she's in the wrong, she needs someone in her corner too. It drove me nuts at first, but then I realized he's right. She needs someone to have her back no matter what, and there is no better man than my dad. I'm glad they have each other.

I lean back in my seat at my mother's dining room table and listen to my grandmother give Brooke shit about her last boyfriend with a smile on my face. Even though she sounds harsh, this is mellow for our grandma, and in truth, she's not wrong. Brooke deserves better than that ass gave her, and she should know it.

I have my sister's infant son, Wesley Jr., asleep over my shoulder. Across the table, my dad has the baby's twin sister, Anna, sleeping in his arms, and next to me in a similar position is my daughter, Hope, on Wes's shoulder. The women sip coffee and cluck over poor Brooke. I listen while Claire tries to diffuse hurt feelings, but really, it is what it is.

This is how our family is—loud, often invasive, and always full of love. I wouldn't have it any other way. So I just sit back and smile, because this is my life with my family, and thank God for that.

two

in the dark

E*yes.*

The smell of sulfur fills my nostrils and smoke sears my lungs. The heavy weight of the rifle in my hands is like second nature to me. I could carry it in my sleep. During training, I probably did.

But it's the eyes that chill me to the bone in the middle of this hot desert.

I don't know how the intel had gone so bad. I know it happens, but not like this. One minute, the mission was going to plan, and the next, the world exploded. Spurts of gunfire can be heard all around me, but it's the screams that ring in my ears.

"Fuck, fuck, fuck!" I hear Adams scream through the comm in my ear. "They're dead. They're all dead."

And he's right. They're all dead. Every last one of

them. I was helpless to prevent this, and still I feel like I should have. It's as bad as if their blood was directly on my hands.

I make my way through the village we've been watching, my heart in my throat. Buildings, homes, the carts in the market, they're all gone, everything is gone. Nothing burned-out shells of what they were before is left behind. And bodies crumpled where they fell. Men, women, children, death does not discriminate. Their eyes vacant after life left them.

If eyes are the window to the soul, then this is a portal to hell as I look at the faces of each person who should not have died. A child we gave a candy bar to yesterday, an old woman who offered coffee in the market, and a beautiful young woman whose belly was swollen with a baby. A baby that would now never be born. Never see their corner of the world, for worse or for better.

Her dark eyes watch me, haunt me, as she sees me and nothing at all. And then they change to the green of Emma's, her belly cut open and our child just gone. I was helpless to stop it. I should have known what would happen. I should have protected them, but I didn't.

The smoke burns my throat as I turn to the left and see Emma's blonde-and-pink hair, her green eyes open and watching me, her beautiful body mutilated, because I was in her life.

"No!" I shout.

But the eyes of the dead scream that this is all my

fault.

"No!" I gasp as my eyes pop open and I awaken.

My head spins as I sit up and put my long legs over the side of the bed. I drop my face in my hands and will the room to stop spinning, but it doesn't.

"Lee?" Emma whispers.

"It's all right, baby," I say without turning to face her. "Go back to sleep."

I feel her delicate hand brush the small of my back, and my breath seizes in my lungs. She wraps her arms around me from behind just before she ducks under my arm and swings around into my lap, dislodging my face from my hands, and I sit up. I hate the worry I see on her beautiful face, and there's a burning in my gut that I put it there.

"I'm okay, honey," I tell her gently. "It's okay. Go back to sleep."

She looks into my eyes for a long moment before she seems to come to some resolve. What, I don't know, but she doesn't make me wait long to find out. Emma presses her mouth to mine. She swipes her tongue over my bottom lip, and I open for her to deepen the kiss.

"What was that for?" I ask her when I pull back to look at her beautiful face in the moonlight that shines through our bedroom window.

"I want to make you feel… more than okay," she answers hesitantly, and then she grinds her hips down over mine. I grit my teeth as all the blood in my body rushes to my dick.

"You don't have to," I tell her, and it's true. We haven't been intimate like this since the baby was born. First, her health was not great, and then she just needed time to heal. The experts say to wait six weeks after a regular delivery before resuming sex, and her delivery was anything but. Not to mention, Emma is going to be my wife, not a nameless body to fuck away my demons. I would never use her like that. She's more—sex with Emma is so much more than just a quick fuck.

"I want to," she says before kissing me again. She rocks her hips back and forth, and the feel of her heat brings my cock to life. I have always wanted this woman. There will never be a time when I don't want this woman. At least not as long as I'm breathing. It feels like all she has to do is wink or swing her lush hips my way, and I'm hard as a rock.

"You're not ready." It's only been two months since she had Hope in the most unconventional way. I don't want Emma to push herself for me. I'm not worth it. Even as hot as she has my body right now, I'd rather go rub one out in the shower than hurt her.

"I'm ready," she says as she raises herself up on her knees, and I feel her opening touch the head of my cock. She's wet, fucking soaked, for me. Centering her pussy over my hard length, she then slowly, oh so fucking slowly, sinks down over me, pulling me inside her. I clench my fists at my sides, terrified that I'll grab her and take her like we both liked before she was hurt.

I can't help the groan that's ripped from my chest as she grips my shoulders tight and begins to ride me in earnest.

"Lee," she gasps as she tips her head back. Her hips rise and fall over mine, and I take the opportunity to pull her nipple into my mouth and swirl my tongue around her peak. "Yes."

I growl as she slams down hard over me and nip at the tip of her breast, making her gasp and clench around my cock. I let her nipple go and drag my lips through the valley between them. I nibble the side of her breast, letting the sting of my bite push her higher before drawing the wounded flesh into my mouth and laving it with my tongue.

She moves faster and faster over me, grasping at a climax that's just out of reach. I can feel her frustration mounting. This isn't like her; before, she would give in to her passion easily. This, I can fix. I grip the lush curves of her ass in my hands and stand, flipping her to her back easily. With my feet braced on the floor, I wrap her long legs around my waist and take her with sure, even strokes.

"Lee, Lee," she pants as she rocks her head from side to side, her long golden waves fanned out on the bed around her, and she's so fucking beautiful in this moment I could stay here forever, just like this.

I glide my palm down her lower belly to between us, where our bodies join together, and I let my fingers slip over her seam where my cock moves inside her. And then I press a fingertip to her clit, and she arches on the bed at my touch.

"That's it," I praise as I circle her center and drive her higher. "Come for me."

"Not without you," she gasps and raises her hips to meet mine.

"Not yet."

"Lee," she pleads, but I'm not ready to come yet. I want to watch her take flight.

I unwrap her legs from around my hips and spread her creamy thighs open like a butterfly. I lean some of my weight on my hands at her thighs, pressing her open to me. She arches her back and bows off the mattress as I slip and slide through her folds, driving deeper and deeper.

She grips the sheets in her hands, and gasps, "Please."

"Touch yourself for me."

Without hesitation, she slips her small hand down her belly to rest between us where my larger one had been. But instead of helping send her over the edge to paradise, I feel her fingertips slide up the base of my shaft where we join.

"Emma," I warn, but she just closes her eyes and smiles like the cat that got her cream as she toys with me.

I slide almost all the way out and pump into her with shallow thrusts, not giving her what she wants.

"I think I told you to touch yourself, not me."

"I like touching you." She pouts, and it's sexy as fuck.

"Don't play with me, Emma," I warn and stress my point by plunging fast and deep into her waiting pussy.

"Yes," she pants. "I like playing with you."

"And I like watching you play with yourself," I counter. "Are you going to give me what I want?"

"Yes." And then she presses the tip of her middle finger to her clit and swirls it. I watch as she rolls her bottom lip into her mouth and bites down while she touches herself, and then I give her what she wants most—my cock—and drive into her.

"That's it," I praise her as I grip her thighs in my hands and fuck her like she wants. "Faster."

She whimpers as she works to get herself off while taking my cock, but I don't let up. I can't. I'm too far gone. To her, to her body, and the way she makes me feel.

"Please," she begs as she continues to move her fingers over her body, faster still. "It's too big. Too much."

"Faster," I push her as I plunge into her over and over, holding her open for us both to give her the release she needs so badly. That I need to give her.

"Yes."

"Hurry." I drive into her again and again.

"Yes." Her fingers move faster. We're both locked into a race to the finish line. She's so close. I can feel in the way she grips my cock tight that she's almost there.

And then, finally, she cries out as she comes.

I move faster, thrusting harder still. I grip her thighs so tight in my fists that I know she'll wear marks from my fingers tomorrow, branding her as mine, and the thought pulls me over the edge after her.

She takes my weight, wrapping herself around me and holding me close to her as we both struggle to catch our breath.

Finally, I haul her back up the bed and pull the covers up over us before I wrap myself around her. She turns to me, just as eager to touch and taste as before, but this time is less frantic. The need for each other is still there, but it's not out of control like it was before.

We trail our hands and our mouths over each other, taking turns and together, and then she parts her thighs for me, and I slip inside, joining us once again. We rock against each other as we kiss and caress. A slow climb up a smooth hill, and then just as sweetly, we fall into bliss together.

I take a deep breath, and then with my girl in my arms, I drift off into a dreamless sleep.

three

the believer

Six months earlier...

"**H**ello?" *I answer the phone as it rings.*

"I-I need you," he stutters. "I can't do this anymore."

"I'll be right there," I tell him, hoping he can't hear the smile in my voice. It pulls across my lips like a Cheshire cat. "Everything is going to be all right."

"Thank you," he says, and the relief is palpable in his tone. Soon, it will all be over, and he will be at peace... or, as I prefer to think, rotting in hell where he belongs.

"See you soon."

I press the red button on the screen of my phone to disconnect the call and clutch the cool block of glass and metal to my chest. I squeeze my eyes tight and pull in a deep breath to center myself.

This is it. This is what I've been waiting for.

I'm ready.

I grab my keys and set my phone down on the table by the front door. Not many people know that one could be easily tracked by the towers their cell phone pings off of as they go. If anyone were to look, I would be in this house all night long. Although, I won't be here much longer. There is much work to be done.

I take my time as I drive across town. I don't need to get pulled over or draw attention to myself, but also, it would be good for him to take a moment and think about what he's done, why this is what's come to pass. It's time for him to pay the piper, and I hope as his time draws near, he realizes why he must pay.

There is no other way.

I won't allow it.

I park several houses down past a cross street, even though it's late at night. I stick to the shadows, avoiding the streetlamps that give off a soft yellow glow around them. My footfalls are soft and sure up the gently sloping steps to the front porch.

I take another deep breath and hold it, letting the oxygen sear my lungs. The pain grounds me. I need to focus on what is to come. It's important that I feel this moment. That I hold it all in and let it change each molecule of my makeup one by one. It needs to repair the damage, the gaping hole inside me.

I raise my fist and gently knock on the heavy wood of the front door.

"It's unlocked," he calls out from within, and his voice croaks. I wonder how much of the sedative I gave him he's taken tonight. More is probably better. But then again, I don't know.

I look down at the doorknob before tucking my hand into the sleeve of my shirt to twist the knob. Even though some of my prints will be found in this house if they look, one can't be too sure.

I slip inside and turn with the door, shutting it as quietly as I can. I flip the lock closed and drop my back-pack by the door. I pull a pair of cream latex gloves out of the zippered pocket on the front and slide my hands into them before making my way through the house.

I find him sitting on the sofa in the family room. He's leaning forward with his wrists braced on his knees. A shiny black gun is held loosely in his hands.

"I don't want to do it," he says. Tears are coursing down his cheeks.

"That's okay."

"But I can't live like this anymore."

"I know you can't," I say softly as I approach him. My movements are slow and measured.

"Where are your meds?" I ask him before looking around.

"On the kitchen counter," he answers. "But they don't work."

"Let's just try one."

I make my way into the small kitchen and spot them immediately. I twist open the orange bottle and dump a bunch out into my palm, looking for a specific one. To the unknowing, it looks like a bunch of capsules, but I know there are some in this bottle with a special blend inside them. And I know what to look for, because I put them there.

I dump the rest on the kitchen counter. I need to set the scene, after all. I fill a glass with water from the kitchen sink and make my way back to the family room. A room that won't see a family in it for some time.

"Here," I say sweetly, handing him the pill and the glass. "Take this."

He takes both from me with a look of gratitude shining in his dark eyes.

"I don't want to…." he starts, the sadness shining in his eyes.

"I know. It'll be okay."

"Please," he pleads. "Help me."

"I will."

I sit next to him on the sofa. His eyes are glassy from the pills I gave him earlier, but he still tracks me. I'm his lifeline and the only one who can save him now. But I won't. What he doesn't know will kill him.

His body is all but completely limp on the sofa when I wrap my hand around his that's holding the gun. He closes his eyes, thinking I'm going to take the weapon from him. Having made the choice to reach out to me for help, it's the logical conclusion. They snap open as I raise his hand to his head and place the gun at his temple.

"Why?" he rasps.

"You know why."

The pills I gave him make it so he can't fight me, can't choose a different path, one we both know he wishes he could. He never should have trusted me with his care, and he knows that now.

"The village."

"Yes," I confirm. He knows what they did, even if he doesn't know who I am. "And I regret that it has to be this way."

"No—"

And then I pull the trigger.

I let his arm with the gun fall to his side, and I stand up. I make my way to the front hallway, careful not to track any blood or footprints through the house. I quickly strip out of my soiled clothes and gloves and bag them in a zippered bag and then in another one. I step into my extra set of clothes and dump the bagged clothing for disposal in my backpack.

I make my way back through the house and slip out the sliding glass door off the kitchen to the patio and out into the night. I quietly slide the door closed and look back at Adam forlornly, because while it was cathartic to take him out of this world, it was over much too quickly, and now I'm left feeling... I don't know, a little... empty.

I let myself out through the gate and make my way back down the quiet streets to where I left my car. I toss my backpack into the trunk and climb into the driver seat.

The night is quiet, and I like it that way. I don't need to turn on the radio to avoid my own thoughts. And as I drive farther and farther away from him, I relive the moment over and over again in my head. The bridge between Maryland and West Virginia is empty tonight as it crosses the Potomac.

I pull over and pop the trunk. There's a plain brick waiting in the trunk along with my backpack. I unzip the pack and drop the brick in with the clothes before zipping it closed again.

And then I pick up the pack by one of the straps and hurl it over the bridge into the waiting river below. I stand there and watch as it slowly sinks to the bottom, never to be seen again.

When it's finally out of sight for good and there's nothing but a few bubbles left popping up at the sur-face, I climb back into my car and head home, where I shower with dish detergent and bleach. I load up my meager belongings, nothing more than what fits into two duffle bags, and then I climb into my car and leave this life behind.

There's one thing for certain. While tonight was a victory, my task is incomplete, and it will remain so as long as they are living.

four

thankful

Present day

"Mm-hmm…" I groan as I open my eyes and see my woman on her knees between my thighs. Her slim hands squeeze my balls and work my shaft, and her blonde curls shimmy as she bobs over me. I can't help but let out another groan as I watch her pretty pink lips slide up and down my cock.

"Mmm," she purrs when her baby-blues meet mine, and I gently brush her hair back from her face to watch her move over and around me.

"I like your idea of a wake-up call, baby," I tell her as I twist my fingers in her hair.

She slides me out of her sweet mouth and then dips her head farther to lick all the way up my hard length.

Her hand doesn't stop as she works me at the base. "I thought you could use a little sweetness to start your day."

"Come here," I growl as she takes me to the back of her throat again only to pull me free once more.

"No, Lee," she says, her voice husky with sleep and sex. "This one's just for you."

"I want you," I growl.

"And you can have me," she says with a saucy wink and a kiss to the very tip of me. "After I suck you off."

And then she dives back down, doubling her efforts as she licks and sucks me. She moves her hand and her mouth faster, sucking harder, and I feel that telltale tingle at the base of my spine when she hollows her cheeks.

"Yes," I growl. "That's it, baby." And I knot my fingers in her hair.

I rock my hips in time with her movements. When she locks her eyes with mine, it's by far the sexiest thing I think I've ever seen. That is until she slips her hand down between her thighs and fingers herself while she sucks me off.

"Oh fuck," I bite out as I buck my hips toward her face. "Fuck, that's sexy. I could watch you get yourself off all day."

"Could you now?" she purrs as her hot-as-hell mouth hovers just over my cock. Her head tips back on her shoulders, and she moans as she pushes herself closer to bliss while she jacks me with her other hand.

"Oh no," I warn with a tug on her hair. "Finish what you start, baby. Don't you dare make yourself come until my tongue is in that pussy."

"I-I can't stop it," she pants as her grip on my dick tightens, and I knife up in the bed and grab her under her arms before twisting at my waist.

I toss Emma back on the bed where I was and grab her by her hips. I bat her hand away and replace it with mine. She's wet, fucking soaked from sucking my cock, and I slip a finger inside her. She pumps her hips against my hand, and I lean over her, covering her body with mine while I take her there.

Emma wraps her arms around my waist, pulling me closer to her, and she presses her mouth against mine. I press my tongue against her lips, and she parts them for me immediately, letting me in, and I fucking love that too.

And then I feel her wrap a small hand around my cock and stroke.

I press my thumb to her clit, and she bucks against me. Her juices drip down, coating me as we work each other.

"Lee," she pants. "I can't stop it.

"Don't stop it," I tell her as I fuck her with my fingers. Her hand tightens around me, and she strokes harder, faster. Her movements become jerky, and I have to fight to hold it back. And just when I think I won't be able to hold on any longer, her beautiful eyes close and her pussy tightens around my fingers, and I watch with amazement as she comes.

And then the hot ropes of my own release lash out between us.

My breath saws in and out of my lungs as I watch her collect herself. When she opens her eyes, I press a swift kiss to her lips and then pull back.

"Well," she says. "That didn't go how I planned."

"Yeah," I say with a soft smile.

"But it was worth it."

"I figured you'd say that," I tell her.

"But now I'm a mess."

I pull back and look at her, my cum spilling down over her belly, and while that's not usually my thing, it's sexy as hell to see her marked by me. Apparently, I'm a little territorial.

"You are," I growl. "But it's sexy as fuck. And now I get to eat you in the shower, since you distracted me and I didn't get to taste you."

"That's not my fault," she mumbles.

"Oh, it definitely was, the way you were working yourself to get off. I couldn't stop myself."

She smiles that mischievous smile, and I scoop her up from the bed and toss her, mess and all, over my shoulder. Emma lets out a squeak as I head for the bathroom.

I let the shower heat up and then rinse us down.

And then I back her up against the stone wall of the shower and drop to my knees. I pull her legs, one by one, over my shoulders and then slowly, under the spray and steam of the hot shower, I eat her until she screams, the sound muffled by the water and the tile walls.

I watch her full breasts heave with each breath, drop her feet to the shower floor, and slide up her body. I press my mouth to hers and kiss her deeply before turning her around to face the wall. She braces her hands against the cold stone and tips her ass back to meet me.

"Yes," she pants when I slide my hard length through her folds and then slowly, oh so fucking slowly, slip deep inside her.

I hold her hips in my hands and rock against her. This time, we come together, much less frantic and hurried than before. We rock like ships on the sea, and then as I feel her walls flutter and squeeze around me, I plant myself deep inside her, and we fall over the edge together.

After we come back down to earth, I slip from her body and gently wash us both. We dry off and get dressed before Hope wakes up and get her ready for another fun-filled day at my parents' house, where we drop her off before driving to the station. We walk through the doors together and then down the hallway, and it's only when I turn to go to my office and she moves to the elevators that will take her to her basement dwellings that we part for the day. And I do it being so fucking thankful that I have Emma and our daughter in my life, because without them, I'd have absolutely nothing.

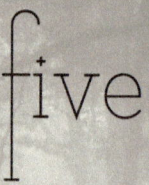five

hear me out

Reports and paperwork. Paperwork and reports. Lather, rinse, and motherfucking repeat.

Some days, I think I will go absolutely out of my mind with all of the paperwork it takes to run this department. As much as I hound the officers that work for me to turn in their reports, I actually hate the thought of paperwork more. But it's my lot in life.

Like the dreams. I can't escape them; my only salvation will be learning to live with them. I had thought I was doing all right, but after Emma was attacked, it's brought them all back tenfold. I can't shut them out anymore.

It's not uncommon that a good cop falls to the demons inside. It happens more often than any of us wish it would. If we stay on the job too long, see too much, eventually, we'll all crave the bite of our own bullet.

Not to mention that PTSD is more common than not in veterans these days. Just look at poor Palmer. He didn't deserve to go out like that. I hate that he did it. I hate that he fell that far and didn't ask for help. He didn't reach out to me or to anyone, but instead, he chose to end his pain once and for all.

And that's what burns in my gut so bad.

With everything I have, every blessing that's been bestowed on me in this life, I can't keep myself from thinking *what if*. What if I ended it all right now? Would the pain go away? Would Emma and Hope be better off without me? Would the rest of my family? The kids? I like to tell myself it won't solve any of the problems, but when I'm so deep in the darkness, I just don't know.

A heavy knock falls at my door.

"Enter," I bark as I rub my temples. The ever-present pounding behind my eyes is building up to its daily crescendo.

I brace as the doorknob turns. The anxiety wells up inside me. I fucking hate it. I hate this uncontrollable feeling of panic that storms inside me every time there is an unknown. It's not normal. I'm not normal.

"Hey, man," Wes says as he pokes his head in my office. I'm actually not surprised he showed up here today. It's Claire's first day back after her maternity leave.

"Hey," I reply. "What's up?"

"I was in the station talking to Claire, and I wanted to pop in and say hi, see what's up before I head back to my office," he says casually. *Too casually.*

"Is that all?" I watch him carefully, and I know without a doubt what I see written on his face even though he doesn't want me to.

"Yeah, of course," he says, letting the door close behind him. "What else would it be?"

"I'm fine, Wes," I tell him on a heavy sigh. "Or I will be."

"Yeah," he agrees. "You will be, but not yet."

"It's fine."

"Look, remember Ames?"

"Yeah," I answer, wondering what he could be going on about. I haven't talked to Ames in years. "What's up with Amy?"

"I ran into him the other day at the gym," Wes says. "He was in a really bad way."

"I'm sorry to hear that," I mumble, because I know exactly how he must have felt, and I'm afraid to ask, because if he lost his way like Palmer, then there's no coming back.

"Me too," Wes says. "But now he's doing great," he finishes, surprising me.

"I'm happy to hear it."

"He said he's seeing this great counsellor out of the VA hospital," he adds. "He said she's amazing and he's never been happier."

"Good to know," I mumble hesitantly.

"Here's his number in case you want to get ahold of him, reach out," Wes tells me as he drops a torn piece of paper with a handwritten number on it on top of my desk.

"I don't know," I start as I lean back in my chair. "I don't know if therapy is for me."

"Just think on it."

"I'm not there yet," I lie. "If it gets bad enough, I'll call."

"Brother," he warns quietly.

"Really."

"The bags under your eyes tell me that it's bad enough."

"It's really not that bad. I'm fine."

"It's time to live your life the way you should," he says quietly. "Fully, no half measures."

"I will."

"Good," he says before walking to my door and pulling it open. "I'm glad to hear it."

"See you around, man."

"See you, Lee," he says. "And remember, live your life."

And then he's gone.

"Fuck," I bite out, running my hand through my hair. He's right. I'm fucked up, but I'm not ready to admit there's a problem yet. I can pull myself back from the brink. I just have to try a little harder.

I lean into my desk and stare at the papers across the battered wood top. I try to focus on the pages, but the words just spin and swirl all over the pages.

I flip my pen end-over-end between my index finger and thumb, but it's no use. I can't help but think, is Wes right? Am I not living my life?

Half measures, he said. Is that me?

A soft knock falls on my office door.

"Enter."

The handle turns, and I brace. Once day, I swear I won't be jumping at ghosts or tilting at windmills. One day, I'll just be able to be. I pull in a harsh breath and let it out slowly, forcing the anxiety that wells up inside me to slowly ebb away.

Emma, in a pair of baby-pink scrub pants and an old Dead Presidents T-shirt, slides through the opening, and my heart beats just a little but faster but in a good way.

"Hey, honey," she says, smiling at me brightly.

"I didn't expect to see you so soon," I tell her.

"Am I bothering you?" she asks me, and I hate the nervous look that fills her face.

"You?" I ask. "Never. I always have time for you. I always want to see you in the middle of my day."

"Okay," Emma says quietly.

"So what's up?"

"Okay," she jumps in, holding up her hands in front of her. "Hear me out, okay?"

"Okay."

"I can't have another baby." The words are like a bomb dropped between us, and I want to diffuse it for her—no, I need to.

"I know, baby, and that's all right," I reassure her. "Hope is everything and then some."

"I know," she says timidly, and timid is not a word I would use to describe my woman normally. "But, what if…"

"What if what?"

"What if the right baby for us came along?" she finishes.

"How so? Like in adoption?"

"Yeah," she agrees. "What if we found out there was a baby who needed a home?"

"Like right now?" I ask, panicking, because we have a newborn in the house already. Two might kill us.

"Yeah," she says. "I'm not saying we force it and go out looking, but think about our profession. If one of us hears of a baby in a situation, maybe we put in to care for that child."

"I don't know," I hedge. "We already have one baby. Two would be pretty hard."

"Wes and Claire seem to be doing all right."

"I don't know."

"It'll be all right," she promises, and in my head, I hear Wes saying *"no half measures."* "I promise."

"Live your life."

"Okay," I agree. "If the right baby comes along, we'll consider it. Together."

"Eeek!" she squeals before running around my desk, grabbing my face in her hands, and then pressing her mouth to mine. All before she spins on her sneakers and leaves my office quicker than she entered it.

I look back down at the papers that are scattered all over my desk, and my eyes catch on the torn piece of paper Wes had set there.

"Live your life."

"What if the right baby for us came along?"

"No half measures."

I pick up the piece of paper and tap its edge on the desk before I grab the phone on my desk and let my fingers dial.

I guess it's time I made a phone call.

It rings once, twice, before he answers, "Hello?"

"Amy?" I reply. "It's Goodie."

"Hey, man. How the hell are you?"

And isn't that the million-dollar question?

six

for her

Three weeks later

"I think you should do it."

"Really?" I ask as I watch her chop up a cucumber and drop it in the big salad bowl on top of the rest of the greens and vegetables Emma has already chopped. Hope is curled up in my arms, babbling her happy baby chatter, just glad to be spending time with her mom and dad.

"Yeah," she says softly.

Emma stops what she's working on to look up at me, and I watch as her face goes soft, but the ever-present worry still flits through her eyes. I hate that I've put that there. I hate that I've caused her any kind of emotion other than happiness and contentment. My gut roils and saliva pools in my mouth, and I nod, just a mindless bob up and down, as I look away.

"Lee," she calls me softly, and I look back to her beautiful face.

"Yeah, honey?" I rasp quietly, my voice seeming stuck in my throat.

"Lee, I love you," she says firmly. "And it's going to be okay. Do you understand what I'm trying to say?"

"Yes."

"I believe in you," she whispers. Tears well up in her pool blue eyes, making my own vision blur a bit. "It's going to be okay."

"Okay," I repeat her words.

"So call your friend."

"All right, honey."

"Do it now," she commands gently. "I'll take Hope."

I look down at my girl who has settled in and slowly started to drift off to sleep in my arms. The weight of her little body grounds me. It keeps me centered. I feel like I can almost do anything, because this little girl will need me to. And for her, I will do it.

"Nah," I reply. "She's happy. I'll take her to the office with me."

"Okay. I'll call you when dinner's ready."

"Thanks."

I make my way out of the kitchen and up the stairs. My office is one of the smaller bedrooms to the back of the house, in between our bedroom and Hope's nursery. She's just about drifted off, and I could put her in her crib, and she would probably be fine, sleep for a bit, but I can't. I need to hold my child.

I push open the door and head toward the big desk in the back. I inherited it from my grandfather's home. He was a police chief before my dad, before me. He was one in a long line of Goodnites who've served this community. It's dark wood with an ornate trim around the edge and the top lovingly battered with years of use.

I kick the chair out and pull my phone from my pocket. I drop it on the desk and sit down before walking the seat back under the desk. Hope squirms and wiggles a bit but drifts back to sleep in her daddy's arms.

I take a deep breath and hold it in, letting the oxygen burn in my lungs before I let it go. I do it again. And then a third time. And then I pick up my phone and slide my finger across the screen to unlock it. I call up the number I saved there three weeks ago when Wes dropped a scrap piece of paper on my desk. I knew I should do it right then, the first time I called. I should have grabbed the rope he was offering me, but I didn't. I couldn't. I wasn't ready. And to be honest, I'm still not. But I can't keep being this person.

I hit the little button to place the call.

It rings.

And rings.

And rings.

And then… he answers.

"Hello?"

"Hey, Amy," I answer and then push out a heavy breath. "I'm ready."

"You won't regret this, brother," he reassures me.

"Yeah," I start. "I don't know about that yet but… I need some help."

"There's a group meeting tomorrow night at seven thirty," he replies. "Don't let this own you."

"Don't say a word."

"I'll be there," I reply before I ask the question that plays over and over in my mind. "Do you ever think about...?"

"Don't say a word."

"All the time. All the fucking time," he says quietly before changing the subject. "I'll text you the address. See you tomorrow night."

And then he ends the call.

I look up when there's a knock at the door. Emma is standing there with a smile on her face. Her hair is a mess piled up on top of her head, and she's in leggings and my sweatshirt. She has two days a week that she works from home unless there's an emergency so that she can be home with Hope, and by the pink in her cheeks and the sparkle in her eyes, she's loving this new arrangement.

"What's up?" I ask.

"I just like looking at you two."

"Well, we are pretty cute," I reply.

"It's true." She laughs. "Plus, I came to tell you dinner's ready."

"I'm ready," I say as I push my chair back to stand up and follow her down the hall.

"How did it go?" she asks. "Your phone call that is." I can tell that she's just as nervous about it as I am. Even though I haven't spoke about it much, I know that she's as nervous and as hopeful as I am. In fact, she might be even more so. She loves me that much. I can't believe that just a year ago, I almost lost my chance at her, at this life. I won't give it up now.

"There's a meeting tomorrow at seven thirty."

"Are you going?" she asks and it sounds like she's walking on eggshells around me. I hate that I've put her so ill at ease.

"Yeah," I answer, and the look of relief on her face just about breaks my heart.

"Good."

"Yeah."

I may not want to do it, but for these two, I will. I would do anything for her, for both of them. Emma and Hope are my entire world, and if they need me to be strong, to be whole again, then I will do my best to get there.

Even if I die trying.

seven

don't say a word

My knees are weak, and my palms are sweaty. I haven't been this nervous in ages. Honestly, it's like a bad Eminem song. But here I am, sitting in my Tahoe outside the VA clinic.

The screen of my phone lights up with an incoming text. It draws my attention to it where it sits in the cupholder next to me, illuminating a picture of Emma and Hope cuddled in the rocker she loves so much. I snapped it early one morning when I woke to find them there together. Emma was singing "Blackbird," and Hope was babbling along. When Emma noticed me standing in the doorway, she laughed and apologized for her terrible singing, but after what we went through, it was one of the most beautiful things I had ever heard, simply because she was alive and able to sing.

It's one of my most favorite pictures. So much so that I set it as my lock screen right away.

I pick it up and slide my finger across the screen, unlocking my phone. I call up my Messages app and read the new text there. It's from Emma, and it gives me the courage I need.

EMMA: You got this, babe. We love you!

She's right. I do have this. I can do this. I can and I will, because they need me to be okay again. And I would do anything for them.

I close my eyes and let my head hang forward. I pull in a deep breath and then push it out. I take in another and another.

And then there's a knock on my window.

My eyes snap open, and I see Ames standing next to my door with a smirk on his face. I haven't seen him in years, but I'd still know him anywhere.

I pull my keys from the ignition and scoop up my phone before grabbing the door handle and pushing it open.

"You coming or what?" he asks with a laugh.

"I'm coming."

"I know," he replies. "I just felt like giving you shit. But for real. This is a good place."

"Thanks. I owe you." And I do. I needed someone

to give me the in to make me go. I needed someone who would give me no excuses and take absolutely none of mine.

"Nah," he says. "I'm just glad you're here."

"Me too."

"Who would like to start tonight?" Jane, the therapist, asks the room, and I freeze. I fucking freeze like a deer in headlights, because I don't know what to say or if I should say anything at all.

"Don't say a word."

"I will," Amy says from his seat next to me. "We made a lot of mistakes. Sometimes, I see each one play out in my head at night, and I can't make it stop."

I close my eyes, because what he's saying, I've experienced firsthand. When I close my eyes, I see murder and mayhem behind my lids, but it's at night, when I'm asleep, that the monsters come out to play with me.

"And how does that make you feel?"

"Like a monster," he says. "Like I'm unworthy, unclean."

"And are you?" she asks.

"Don't say a word."

Ames pauses for a moment before answering, and I think he's going to say yes and affirm that he is the monster he thinks he is, that we all are, but he doesn't.

"No, I'm not."

I'm not going to lie; sometimes, I wonder if we were trained too well. Am I nothing but a killer? Did the warrior take over the man? I don't know. I just don't fucking know.

"And how did you come to that conclusion?"

"A lot of soul searching and the help of this group."

"Good," she says after a beat. "That's what we're here for."

"Thanks for that," Ames says.

"Is there anyone else who would like to share tonight?"

"Don't say a fucking word."

I hear the captain's words over and over in my head. The command from that long-ago night rings out over and over, and it's at war with my need to find help and healing. Can I keep my promise and still be a better man for my fiancée and daughter?

"Anyone?"

I raise my hand.

"Yes?" she calls on me as her eyes lock in on fresh meat. I watch her pupils flare when she takes me in. A few years ago and I would have been all about the invitation in her eyes—whether she was my new therapist or not—but now, I'm a one-woman man.

"My name is Lee, and I was in the navy."

"And what did you do in the navy, Lee?" she asks

me. Her voice is quiet and almost melodic as she asks her probing questions.

"I can't talk about that."

"Would you like to share with us, Lee?"

"No," I answer and watch the disappointment on her face. "But I will anyway, because it's the right thing to do."

"Good," she praises. "Go on."

"I see their eyes at night," I begin.

"Whose eyes?"

"The eyes of the dead. But they see me, and I can't get away from them."

"How does this make you feel?" she asks, and I surprise myself by uttering the only answer I can.

"Terrified."

eight

true believer

Fate. It has to be fate.

Just like a fly in a spider's web... he came to me. I didn't have to plot or scheme to get him here. He came willingly to me. I watched him from across the parking lot, wondering if my luck could be that good tonight, and it was. He was there. He was really there.

I could have pinched myself.

I watched and waited all night for him to speak, to share, and when he did, it was beyond my wildest imagination. He wasn't ready to share the whole story yet, but I know that he will. And soon. We're both living with the ugly truth of his actions, his negligence, and soon it will all come to fruition.

After all, I haven't waited this long for the truth

only to be disappointed.

A true hunter enjoys the time they spend stalking their prey before they go in for the kill. And I will savor this hunt.

But when he said he was terrified... I swear I could almost smell the fear that would come from him by the time I was done with him on his skin, in the room.

But I know I have to wait.

It's not his time yet.

But when it is...

I got you.

Because I am the True Believer after all.

nine

old ghosts

"So?" Emma asks the minute I walk through the door. "How did it go?"

"Good," I answer. "Were you waiting for me?"

"Nooo," she answers. "Yes, obviously." She rolls her beautiful eyes at me.

Emma was sitting on the sofa in the living room when I walked through the front door. The lights are turned down low, and the television is on the lowest volume possible so not to disturb Hope's sleep. She looks as if she was reading on her tablet, but the minute the lock turned, her ears honed in on me.

"You look comfy," I say, taking in her ridiculous amount of fuzzy blankets and thick socks. I wedge my body between the back of the sofa and her so I can pull her into my arms.

"That's because I am, silly. Now spill."

"It was good." I smile at her. "I didn't share much, but I shared."

"Good."

"I feel... I don't know. Almost like a weight has been lifted," I admit.

"That's great, honey."

"She asked me if I wanted to see her for private therapy sessions," I add. "She thinks that might make a bigger difference."

"Okay," Emma says hesitantly. "How do you feel about that?"

A chuckle bubbles up from my chest, because in that moment, she sounds so much like Jane during the group session.

"What?" she asks.

"That's what the therapist asks everyone over and over. 'How does that make you feel?' So it made me laugh when you said it too. I guess I didn't realize what a mess I had become."

"You're not a mess, Lee," she says softly.

"Sometimes, it feels like it."

"You're not a mess," she repeats.

"Okay."

"So what are you going to do?" she asks.

"I'm going to try it out."

"Good," she says, and her smile is brighter this time.

"There's something else I want to try out," I tell her.

"Oh yeah, what's that?"

"I think I want to make out on this couch with my fiancée for a bit, and then I think I'm going to eat her, and then I'm going to carry her to bed. What do you think?"

"I think it's worth a shot."

"You never know until you try," I tell her just before I cover her body with mine and get busy trying a whole bunch of things.

"This was a major fuck-up."

Our commanding officer is pissed and rightfully so. This is a shitfuck of epic proportions. Our intel said the terrorist was hiding in the village, but when we got there, they were all dead.

"This op went so far FUBAR it's not remotely repairable!" he keeps yelling.

We all stand silent, huddled around him.

"What do you want us to do now?" Ames asks.

"Nothing. Not one fucking thing."

"But—" Donovan starts.

"I said nothing," he growls in Rick's direction.

Ghost shoots him a look to tell him to shut up and back down before he finds his ass in a sling. Our CO is and has always been wound just a little too tight. He's not my favorite SEAL, but the team is where I belong, so I have to put up with his bullshit like everyone else.

"They were all dead when we got there," CO explains—something we all know all too well in a way that the eyes of the dead will haunt me in my sleep. Not only was everyone dead, but so was my informant and her daughter.

I should have protected them, and I didn't.

And I'm going to have to live with that for the rest of my life. That is, if I make it out of the desert in one piece. Donovan seems to be on a one-man suicide mission since his wife left him, and Ghost is determined to take us all with him to protect his crazy ass. But this was more than that.

We made a mistake—a fatal mistake—and it cost hundreds of innocent people, including women and children, their lives.

"So that's what we're sticking with."

"But—" Palmer starts.

"No buts," CO shouts. "Don't say a word. Don't say a fucking word. Do you understand me?"

"Yes, CO," we all reply.

"Not one fucking word or it'll be your asses in the

wind, not mine," he growls, and something burns in my gut. And then he looks right at me, his mean eyes locked on mine, and the words he shares next I know are meant for me and me alone. And it's also me who will have to carry them with me for the rest of my days. "It's your hands that hold their blood."

"Yes, CO."

"Don't say a word."

I gasp as I come awake. The CO's words are still ringing in my ears. I sit up in bed, kicking my legs over the side of the bed as my breath saws in and out of my lungs and my hands dig into the skin at my thighs. The stinging pain grounds me and holds me to the now, while the last tethers of my dream still hold me down.

"Lee?" Emma says softly, sleep making her voice husky as she calls out for me.

"I'm okay," I tell her, but am I? Really? I know I told her that I was after last night's meeting, but am I really? I make a mental note to call Jane in the morning and set up a time to meet with her. If I can squash this in the bud, then maybe my lies to Emma aren't so bad. I know it's wrong the minute I think the words, but I'm already down the tracks. I can't stop the lies, the covering. I'm too far gone. I don't know which is worse, the fact that I'm so fucked up in the head or that I'm afraid to let the knowledge weigh down on Emma. I just hope that in the end, I can make it right.

I turn back to the bed, take Emma in my arms, and

hold her tight. She settles into me, and I love the feel of her there. I would do anything, say anything, to keep her here. I almost lost her twice, and I won't ever do it again. I'll die fighting. So I lie again.

"Really, I'm okay," I tell her. "Let's go back to sleep."

"Okay, baby."

And then just like that, Emma settles into me even more and drifts back to sleep. Her trust in me is so profound that the lies I've told keep me from finding peace for hours longer. It's a blind trust that I know that I don't deserve. I vow to put these old ghosts to rest once and for all, because if I can't, I just might lose everything in the process, and I know without a doubt I won't survive that.

I can only hope now that it's not too late.

ten

benjamin

I thought about Emma all through my drive to the station. It was easy to keep my focus on her as she was babbling happily about babies and how many she wants on the drive there. But what had my thoughts spinning was my inability to give her the moon.

"You okay?" she asked when we pulled into the lot, her hand resting gently on my forearm.

"Of course," I said with a smile, my lies getting deeper and deeper. One day, they'll bury me alive if I don't stop it.

I walked her to the elevator and kissed her deeply before letting her go for the day. "I'll see you later."

And then she was gone. Down to her basement morgue where she does all the creepy things I definitely don't want to think too long and hard about.

So I turned on my heels and stalked down the hallway to the kitchenette, lost in my own thoughts. I poured myself a cup of coffee and then made my way into my office, unlocked the door, and flipped on the lights. I set my coffee down on my desk and booted up my computer, sipping the hot tar while I waited. Even coffee in the desert was better than the gray water we brew here. But it does the job.

I open my email and scroll through the reports that have been filed. There's nothing pressing here. And as I flip through page after page, all I see are the lies I've been telling. I can't see past them anymore, so I close out my email and finish my coffee before pushing the cup to the corner of my desk, out of the way.

I open the first file in my inbox on my desk, when there's a knock at the door.

"Enter!" I call out, and Wes walks in.

"How's it going?" Wes asks as he makes his way into my office and sits in one of the chairs in front of my desk.

"Same old, same old. Just living the dream," I tell him.

"Good," he says, and then he watches and waits. "So... how did it go?"

I let out a sigh. "Good. The therapist told me she would be open to taking me on as a private patient."

"What do you think?"

"Maybe," I say, shrugging, and there come more

lies pouring out of my good-for-nothing mouth.

"What does Emma think?"

"Emma thinks I should do it," I answer.

"Maybe it's not a bad idea," Wes says casually.

"You think?"

"I think whatever you need to do to win the fight—I don't care what it is. Claire wouldn't be who she is if you hadn't forced her to start seeing the department shrink."

"And look where that got us," I snap, letting all the ugly fill me from inside out.

"You have to let it go once and for all," he tells me, and I know he's not wrong.

"I know; you're right."

"Then get help."

"I will."

"Good," he says as he pushes up from the chair in front of my desk. "Remember what I said. No half measures."

And then he's gone, and I get back to work.

It's long past lunchtime, and I'm back in my office when my phone rings.

"Goodnite," I answer.

"Captain Goodnite, this is Selma Harris with Brick

Township Child Protective Services," the woman on the other end of the line says.

"And what can I do for Brick Township?" I ask. "We're not exactly near you."

"I have on record with the state of New Jersey that two weeks ago, you and your wife, Emma Parker Goodnite, submitted paperwork to be put on the list for prospective adoptees." And when she says that, my breath seizes in my lungs. It can't possibly be that easy.

"Yes," I whisper.

"This afternoon, a twenty-year-old mother over-dosed on heroin in an alley. She left behind a seven-month-old son," she says. "By some miracle, he is healthy and happy."

"What does this have to do with my wife and me?"

"This little boy has absolutely no one. No father or grandparents, not even distant aunts or uncles to take him in. So I'm left with a job to do. One that is often difficult and sad. Where I watch more children go into the system than to happy families. So imagine my surprise when I see that a decorated police captain from another township and his doctor wife check all the boxes and are on the list for a child."

I don't say anything. I can't. I can't find my voice. It's only been two weeks. When Emma and I filled out the paperwork, we thought that it would be months at the very minimum but most likely years before we had a baby placed with us. I feel hope well up inside me that I can do this; I can give this to Emma, the woman I love more than anything in this world, the woman who once dreamed of a huge family full of love and babies with me until the possibility was stolen from us. Can it really be this easy? Can I give this to her?

"So I'm left with a decision," she says. "I can place this baby in the system, or I can take the opportunity to give him two loving parents, a little sister, and a huge extended family of veritable heroes. So if you were me, what would you do?"

"He's really ours?" I whisper.

"His name is Benjamin."

Panic surges through my body when I hang up the phone with Mrs. Harris. It feels like every synapse is not only firing but also on fire. I close my eyes tight and will my body to calm down, but it's no use.

The vision of Emma flayed open on the living room rug flashes behind my eyelids. I hear a baby cry. I can smell the coppery tang of her blood as it fills the air.

Can we really handle another baby?

And what if she's right? What if Emma and I are the best shot Benjamin has at a good life? Can I be the one to deny him that? Or Emma the opportunity to be a mother again?

Fuck me, we're having another baby. Only this one is seven months old and has no biological family left.

I take a deep breath, and then another, and then another. I hold the air in my lungs until it burns, and then I slowly expel it. I just sit at my desk and breathe in and out and take inventory of each inch of my spine and every muscle in my body.

When I can focus again, I push up from my desk and make my way to the door. I know what I need to do. I slide my cell phone from my pants pocket and quickly type out a text to Wes.

> ME: I need you to hold down the fort here. Something came up.

I watch as the little bubble pops up, letting me know he's typing.

> WES: A case?

I quickly respond.

> ME: No, personal.

> WES: Good, I hope.

> ME: All good. Just make sure my sister doesn't burn down my station while I'm out.

WES: WILCO.

WILCO, or will comply Wes replies, letting me know that he's got my back and my sister won't be allowed to wreak havoc while I'm out of the county. Wes is a good man, my brother in every sense of the word and I know he would be there for me when I needed him. He's probably the only man I would ever let marry my kid sister, whether she's a menace or not. Which she is.

ME: Emma and I are leaving early. Be back tomorrow.

WES: Roger that.

And just like that, I know everything here is covered.

I calmly walk down the hallway to the elevator, even though on the inside I'm a riot of emotions and thoughts and feelings. I press the call button and count the seconds until the steel doors open with a ding.

I press the button for the basement and take a deep breath as the doors close me in. I lean on a hand against the cool metal wall of the elevator. I need to get my shit together, because when these doors open, Emma will see me right away. So I roll my shoulders back as the descent slows and then eventually comes to a stop.

The doors open, and I step out into her basement dwelling. There's a reason why Claire calls it her lair, because it's made up of old brick walls and fluorescent lights, and it's also a morgue and laboratory.

"Lee?" she says with a smile as she looks up and sees me. "What are you doing here?"

It's only a little past lunchtime, and most days, Emma and I leave each other to our duties while we're at the station. Having worked together for years before we found our way together, we're used to coexisting in the same building without having to be constantly near each other. So for me to show up here for no reason is not completely unheard of, but it's also not common-place either.

"I have some news," I tell her right away. I let my legs eat up the distance between us.

"What is it?" she asks, suddenly nervous. I under-stand her reaction; we haven't had the easiest road to date, and it's still pretty damn rocky on the day-to-day.

I pull her into my arms. "I heard from a social worker in Brick Township."

"I don't understand," she replies as she tips her head to the side and purses her pink lips. I press my mouth to hers in a soft but swift kiss and then explain.

"She saw our application for adoption and wanted to talk."

"Lee…." Emma whispers.

"This morning, a young woman overdosed, leaving behind a seven-month-old son. He has no biological family to claim him, and Mrs. Harris made it clear we were her first choice."

"Can you tell me about him?"

"All I know is that he's a seven-month-old boy and his name is Benjamin, and if your heart is open to it, we can get in the car right now and go meet him. They've fast-tracked us because of who we are."

"I'll get my bag."

eleven

dreams come true

The ride into Brick was a long one fraught with nervous anticipation. The first thing we did once we were buckled into the Tahoe was call my parents.

"Hello?" my dad answered what seemed like as soon as Emma hit Dial on her phone and the speaker button.

"Hey, Dad," I replied. "It's Emma and me."

"What's up? It's not like you to call midday."

"Everything is fine, but we need to know if Hope can stay with you a little longer than normal. We'd really appreciate it."

"Of course," he responded immediately. "You know I love my baby girl, but what's going on?"

Emma looked to me for confirmation. I nod, because if we're leaving the beach with another baby, it's going to be all hands on deck. Everyone in the family is going to need to know what's going on.

"Are you ready?" Emma asked my dad.

"Of course."

"You tell him, Lee," she said, and I could see she was practically bouncing in her seat with excitement.

"Tell me what? I'm dying here, guys," My dad says through the line.

"I got a call from Brick Township today," I answered. "They have an orphaned boy they'd like us to foster to adopt."

"Lee," my dad whispered, and I could hear the emotion that filled his gruff voice. He of all people knew how much a big family had meant to Emma and me and how much it had hurt when that dream was snatched away.

"We're going meet him now," I tell him, letting him hear the emotion, the excitement in my own voice.

"What's going on?" I heard my mother ask. "Liam?"

"It's Lee and Emma," he replied. "They're getting a boy placed with them tonight."

"Oh God," she cried, and I felt my own tears well up in my eyes.

"Go get our boy, Lee," my dad said. "We've got Hope safe with us."

"I will. Thanks, Pop."

And then he rang off.

After that, we pulled into a Target and bought a car seat, some blankets, some pajamas, and clothes, but not too much, because we didn't really know what size he is or how much he's going to need. Emma had sorted things in the trunk before making a little stack of board books and toys we grabbed on the fly next to where I was installing the rear-facing seat.

After that, we hit the road again.

Now, the sun is setting as we pull into Brick Township. My heart is beating so hard in my chest that it wouldn't surprise me if Emma can hear it too. She's fidgeting in her seat. She's so nervous she's about to bounce right out of the car door.

"It's going to be okay," I tell her quietly as I take her hand in mine and place it on my thigh.

"What if we don't get him?" she asks.

"It's going to be as it's supposed to be."

"What if someone else claims him?"

"Then we pray those people are better for him than we are and that he's exactly where he's supposed to be."

"What if something's wrong?" she asks. "I know you said the mother was an addict."

"Then we love him the best of our abilities, and a mother who is a doctor that will watch over him like the mama bear she is would not be a bad thing."

"You're right," she says. "We're going to love

him."

"We're going to love him."

"Thank you," she says softly.

"For what?" I ask, and like a sock to the gut, she answers me.

"For making all my dreams come true."

The way she loves me, after all we've been through, after all I've put her through, brings me to my knees every time. If it's the last thing I do on this earth, I'll make sure she feels the depth of how very much I love her.

I pull into the parking lot of their social services offices and park the car. I suck in a deep breath and then pull my keys from the ignition and step down from the driver seat before walking around and opening the door for Emma. I hold my hand out to her, and she takes it.

"It's going to be okay," I say again, smiling as I look into her beautiful blue eyes.

"Okay," she repeats with a smile of her own.

I hold her hand as we walk through the lot and into the building that looks like every other building I've ever been in that was used by a governmental agency of some kind with its beige, nondescript walls and utilitarian carpet.

"Are you the Goodnites?" an older woman sitting at the front desk asks.

"Yes, we are."

"I'll call Selma down now," she says before picking up her phone and dialing a number.

"Thank you," Emma replies softly.

"Selma, the Goodnites are here," she says into the phone before hanging up. "She'll be down any second."

"Thank you."

"It's not every day we get to see a fairy tale happen for one of these kids," she adds.

"You must be Dr. Goodnite," a Hispanic woman says as she steps into the room. She's about my mother's age and still beautiful. Her brown hair is liberally streaked with silver, and there are pleasant lines around her eyes that say she smiles and does it a lot. "And you must be Captain Goodnite."

"Lee," I reply, shaking her hand.

"Of course. I'd know you anywhere. You're as handsome as your picture in the paper."

"Quit flirting, Selma," the other woman admonishes with a laugh.

"No," she says with a broad smile on her face. "Life's too short not to have any fun and especially on such a good day."

"Sure enough," the woman replies.

"Now," Selma says, clapping her hands. "Would you like to meet Benjamin?"

"More than anything," Emma breathes.

"Then let's get to it," she says. "My tiny man is awaiting. If you'll follow me."

We follow Selma as she unlocks a set of doors with her name badge and then down a long hallway. Finally, at the end of it, where it dead-ends at another hallway, we turn to the right, and then she pulls open a door to an office and holds it for us.

And I stop dead in my tracks, and so does Emma, because seated behind the desk is another woman, and in her arms is the most beautiful baby boy I have ever seen. He's bouncing and giggling on her lap as she holds him. His mocha-colored skin is smooth and looks soft to the touch, and he has bright hazel eyes that are shining in his merriment. His head is topped with a riot of short, dark-brown curls, but it's his wide smile with two tiny teeth poking out that light up the whole room.

And I know without a doubt in my mind or in my heart that this is my son.

"This is Benjamin," Selma says. "Amber, these are the Goodnites."

"Would you like to hold him?" Amber asks Emma.

"Can I?" she responds as if someone offered to let her wear the Hope Diamond, and I don't blame her one bit, because I feel the same way.

"Of course," Selma answers. "He's yours."

"Really?" Emma breathes, and I look from where Benjamin is now cradled in her arms to the social worker.

"Paperwork was fast-tracked for you," she answers with a smile on her face. "We still have some steps to go through, a home visit for one, but otherwise, he'll be yours officially in six months' time. The meeting with the judge will be on the ninth."

"Thank you," I rasp as I reach out and rest my hand on Benjamin's back.

"I love when cases end like this, so thank you."

"I'm going to be your daddy, Benjamin. Is that all right with you?" I ask him, and he gives me his toothy smile again.

"You will be free to change his name once the adoption goes through," Selma says. "He had no middle name, and his last name can also be changed."

"I don't know," I say to the baby. "Benjamin is a good, strong name. How does Benjamin Goodnite sound? Ben? Benny?"

"I love it," Emma agrees. "His birth mom gave him that name, and I think we should honor her with that."

"I agree."

"Benjamin Liam Goodnite," Emma whispers. "Because a good man needs a good, strong name to grow into and lots of good men to look up to."

I choke back the emotion in my voice. I had never thought about having a son to carry on my name the way I carried on my dad's until now, and there is nothing I want more in the world than to be able to give that to this baby—our baby.

"Now, it's a ways back to George Washington Township, so you all better hit the road," Selma says. "We'll be seeing you soon."

"Let's go meet your sister, Ben," I tell him, and then I lead Emma and our son out to the car, where we carefully strap in our precious cargo in the back seat. Emma chooses to ride back there with him so he's not alone, but once we get to my mom and dad's, he'll have Hope with him.

We hit a drive-thru on the way home and grab a couple burgers we eat in the car. Emma mixes a bottle of formula for the baby that they handed us on the way out the door.

He's asleep by the time we pull into my parents' driveway, and just before the front door opens and my family pours out to meet our new son, I look to Emma's smiling face in the rearview mirror and think for the first time in a long time that dreams really do come true.

Eyes.

The smell of sulfur fills my nostrils, and smoke sears my lungs. The heavy weight of the rifle in my hands is like second nature to me. I could carry it in my sleep. During training, I probably did.

But it's the eyes that chill me to the bone in the middle of this hot desert.

I don't know how the intel had gone so bad. I know it happens, but not like this. One minute, the mission was going to plan, and the next, the world exploded. Spurts of gunfire can be heard all around me, but it's the screams that ring in my ears.

"Fuck, fuck, fuck!" I hear Adams scream through the comm in my ear. "They're dead. They're all dead."

And he's right. They're all dead. Every last one of them. I was helpless to prevent this, and still I feel like I should have. It's as bad as if their blood was directly on my hands.

I make my way through the village we've been watching, my heart in my throat. Buildings, homes, the carts in the market, they're all gone, burned-out shells of what they were before. And bodies crumpled where they fell. Men, women, children, death does not discriminate. Their eyes vacant after life left them.

If eyes are the window to the soul, then this is a portal to hell as I look at the faces of each person who should not have died. A child we gave a candy bar to yesterday, an old woman who offered coffee in the market, and a beautiful young woman whose belly was swollen with a baby.

Her dark eyes watch me, haunt me, as she sees me and nothing at all. And then they change to the green of Emma's, her belly cut open and our child just gone. I was helpless to stop it. I should have known what would happen. I should have protected them, but I didn't.

The smoke burns my throat as I turn to the left and

see Emma's blonde-and-pink hair, her green eyes open and watching me, her beautiful body mutilated, because I was in her life.

"No!" I shout.

But the eyes of the dead scream that this is all my fault.

I gasp awake as the eyes of the mother are burned onto the backs of my eyelids. Her unseeing gaze is forever seen in my mind, and I can't escape it. And yet, somehow, it's mingled with Hope and Emma. There's so much blood on my hands, and I know I'll never get clean again.

I kick my legs over the side of the bed, careful not to wake Emma. She's sleeping peacefully next to me. It's the contented sleep of a happy mama with all her cubs tucked in down the hall, all under her roof. And I don't want to disturb that with my nightmares.

My stomach roils and the room spins the second my feet hit the thick Berber carpet. The acid rises up from my stomach and into my esophagus. It burns. Like so many things I did wrong, it burns in my gut, in my throat. I try to choke it back, but it's no use.

My feet race to the bathroom. I swallow over and over again, but the saliva pools in my mouth. I lean over the sink and spit. And then I spit again and again. There's no stopping it.

I drop to my knees on the tile floor in front of the toilet and heave the contents of my stomach until there's nothing left to purge. I hate feeling like this. I hate throwing up. I feel out of control whenever I do. I can't stop it no matter how hard I try.

I spit one last time before I rip off a square of toilet paper and wipe my mouth. I drop it in the bowl and flush. On shaky legs, I climb to my feet and rinse my mouth out with water from the sink.

I'm too wired. I know I won't be able to sleep yet, so I don't bother going back to bed. When I pass through the bedroom, Emma is still sound asleep, tucked under the blankets.

I make my way down the hall to where the babies are sleeping. We decided when we got home last night that for the time being, the kids should be in the same room. And with having two infants under the same roof, it made sense to have all the clothes and diaper changing supplies in one place. Not to mention, they need to get used to being a family. All of us do, really.

Emma and I hoped to have a big family that was close to one another, and now we will.

Quietly, I push open the door to the nursery. We didn't have time to stock the room with furniture and extra baby supplies yet. Tomorrow will mean a trip to the big box baby stores for all the gear like more car seats, diapers, a crib, and a double stroller. But for now, Hope is in her crib, and Benjamin is in the travel crib next to hers. They're both wrapped up in their blankets and encased in footie jammies, and pacifiers in their mouths while they skip clouds in the sky off in their dreamland adventures.

What beautiful faces free of worries and fears. We may end up having a long row to hoe with Benjamin and anything he may have had to overcome in his short life, but we'll do it. He's my son, and she's my daughter. I know it down to my very bones.

The visions of my dream flash through my mind again, and I have to hold onto the doorjamb for support. The vision of all I should have protected and didn't flip through along with Emma and Hope. I almost lost them. What if I can't protect my family? What if I fail them like I have everyone else?

All I know is I can't let that happen. I won't if it's the last thing I ever do. Tomorrow, I'll make time to call my new therapist and set up a time to talk. I have to get it together.

Until then, I'll watch my babies sleep just a little longer before I head back to my room and join their mother. And hopefully, I'll be able to find the peace they so easily do, knowing I do my best to give them their piece of the peace they all deserve so much.

twelve

patience and virtues

Patience.

It's never been one of my natural talents. I hate waiting, and I love to see results right away. And isn't that just so American, the idea that instant gratification is not only needed but deserved? I guess I'm a real American now.

But I also have learned to savor the moment of victory.

For years, I wanted the only person to ever love me to bravely protect her family and her people. And when she was out of options and out of time, she did what she thought was right and put her own safety on the line to help the side of good and right.

But what good did it do when she ended up dead?

How could it be right that she was taken from the

world? From me? When such ugliness prevails?

The winners of the world are not right or good; they are just the strongest bullies. Bullies who convince those that their lives should be forfeit for the right to prevail, but it's all lies.

The world is built on lies, and I know that firsthand.

I have witnessed it time and time again.

But not anymore. This time, I'm going to be the winner.

I take the pink lipstick off the shelf in my study and draw a slash through the picture pinned to the wall in the long line of all the others. I've waited long enough. It might not be time for Goodnite to pay for his crimes yet, but Jonathan Ames just ran out of luck.

It's time to set the wheels of justice in motion again.

I'm ready for him to meet his maker.

Vengeance is mine.

thirteen

jogging strollers and group sessions

The first streaks of gray light cross the early morning sky when I hear Benjamin babbling over the baby monitor. I haven't gone back to sleep yet. The different emotions are at war in my mind, and I couldn't shut them down, so I gave up about an hour ago and just watched Emma sleep.

I gently pull the covers back and kick my legs over the side. I grab a pair of soft gray sweatpants from the chair in the corner of the room and slide them up my legs.

Gently, I shut the door behind me so as not to wake Emma, and then I quietly make my way down the hall to the nursery. When I peek my head inside, Ben is standing in his travel crib, smiling his toothy grin at me.

"Morning, bud," I greet him quietly as I scoop him up to change his diaper. "Let's try to be quiet so we don't wake your sister."

I lay him down on the pale-gray painted changing table that matches Hope's crib. We had chosen gender neutral furniture so it would accommodate any babies that came after her. Fortunately, now we can just add another crib and another dresser, and we might be good.

I unzip his footie jammies and pull his legs free, tucking the material up his back. Two months of being a new dad has taught me to be wary of poop blowouts. Like an IED, they can come from any direction. I pull open the tape on the front, open his diaper, and hit the deck like my life depends on it, because as soon as the cool morning air hit his skin, Ben pisses across the room with the propulsion of a fire hose. This is not something I was prepared for.

"Whoa there, Ben," I tell him when I cover him back up again. "Give a guy a warning next time, won't you?"

Ben just giggles. A soul-soothing sound you wouldn't expect from a child whose mother just died. But then again, Ben is a baby. He doesn't understand. And while he's generally a happy child, some things are bound to pop up from time to time. It's just something we're going to have to keep an eye out for.

I swap out his diaper for a fresh one and tuck his legs back in his jammies. When I scoop him back up, my little princess is chattering away in her crib.

"Well, good morning, sunshine girl," I say as I drop Ben back in his travel crib for a second while I change Hope, and he lets out a squeal of complaint, but otherwise, that's it from him. She smiles at me when I pick her up. "Just don't piss on me too."

Again, Ben just laughs.

I quickly follow the same steps as I did when I changed Ben, but this time, no one pees on me. I bundle her back up in her jammies and scoop her up and lay her over my shoulder, and then I reach down and swoop in for Ben.

"Okay, troops. Who wants breakfast?"

I carry my load of babies down the stairs and lay Hope in her bouncer and set Ben on the floor at my feet while I grab bottles from the counter and the formula from the cabinet. When I turn around, Ben is gone.

"Shit."

Apparently, seven-month-old babies do things like crawl and move a lot faster than an almost two-month-old led me to believe. Fortunately, he didn't make it very far. So I scoop him up in my arms and carry him back around the island in the kitchen.

I mix up the bottles and hand him one while I sit down next to him with Hope in my arms and help her with hers. A couple of highchairs are definitely getting added to the baby gear we need list.

He holds it himself, and I think about all the firsts we missed with him and all the nexts and lasts his biological mother won't ever get to see. It's sad; it's so fucking sad for everyone, and I make a silent vow to Ben and to God that I will do my best by him, that I'll give him the moon and the stars. A wagon and a swing set and even a dog when he's older. A boy should have a dog to go on adventures with.

I look to Hope. She'll have the same. The two of them will be thick as thieves. Double the trouble with kids so close in age. There were eight years between Claire and me, and she followed Wes and me all over. I guess I shouldn't have been surprised when I found out my baby sister fell in love with my best friend. I can only hope these two love each other like Claire and I do.

And then add to that their twin cousins, and the four of them can take on the world. They'll have it better than we did. Claire and I had the best parents in the world, and we still do, but all that love didn't stop a monster from kidnapping and abusing Claire when she was no more than a baby herself. Will I be able to protect them like I couldn't protect Claire? The thought of anyone harming either of my babies has me sick to my stomach. How crazy is it that I've only known these two for such short amounts of time and I already know I would lay down my life for theirs? I would trade my last breath for their next, and I would do it gladly.

"He's going to want some real food in a bit," Emma says from the doorway, and I look over my shoulder to see her in my T-shirt and a pair of leggings. Her hair is tousled, and her skin is still pink from the warmth of the blankets. The combination is sexy as hell.

"Real food?" I ask, surprised. "He's a baby and babies drink milk, either from boobs or bottles, right? Like he and I aren't going to run to McDonald's for a Big Mac and a Coke, right?"

"Yeah." She laughs. "Babies his age eat real food. But no, not a Big Mac and a Coke. At least not yet anyway."

"Really?" I'm just so surprised. There is so much I still don't know about raising babies and being a dad. It's a terrifying experience.

"Yeah."

"Like what?"

"Like baby oatmeal or scrambled eggs," she replies.

"We don't have baby oatmeal, do we?" I ask.

"No, but Selma said he loves scrambled eggs," she replies.

"You better take Hope here while I make the eggs for everyone," I tell her as I start to stand up. At least I can do that for my kid. Having been a bachelor for forty years, I excel at eggs of most varieties.

"I can make the eggs," she tells me. "Plus, you're sexy as hell sitting there with the kids."

"I am, but that doesn't change the fact that your eggs are absolute shit, baby," I say with a laugh.

"Hey!" She pouts. "That is not true!"

"It's true." I laugh as I pass her Hope. "They fed us better in boot camp."

"Now that's just cold," She gripes.

"Would you rather eat my eggs and bacon or yours?" I ask on a raised brow.

"Just shut up and get to cooking for me!" She laughs as she takes my seat with our daughter in her arms. She looks down at Ben sitting on the floor. "We really need some highchairs here."

"I was thinking that just a few moments ago," I agree. "We're going to have to hit the baby stores to-day."

"Now you're speaking my love language."

"You are so weird."

"Hey, throw in a Target run too, and I'll be eating more than your bacon later." She cackles.

"Woman!" I shout. "Don't you go making promises you can't keep."

"Oh, I'm promising." She winks. "I'll see you after bedtime."

"You're going to make me burn my bacon if you don't quit it," I tell her as I flip them in the pan.

"Don't you know it."

And I laugh as I get to work making my family breakfast, which both mother and son love as I knew they would, because my eggs are the shit.

After we eat and I clean up the kitchen while Emma gets the kids dressed and packed up for the day, I play with them in the living room while she showers and dresses. I'll grab a quick shower when she's done.

And then the doorbell rings.

"Who do you guys think that could be?" I ask the kids. They just look at me.

I get up and look out the window next to the door and see my entire family standing on the front porch. My parents, Claire and Wes, their kids, Brooklyn, and Seth. Even my grandma, and I'm not entirely sure she likes me.

"What are you guys doing here?" I ask as they storm into the house.

"Did you think I could keep them away from the new baby for more than a day?" my dad asks with a laugh. My grandmother is yelling in Italian at my mother. One is holding Ben, the other holding Hope.

"Don't you talk to me like that, you crazy old cow!"

"You take that back right now!"

"No."

"You better go intervene," I tell my dad, and he just laughs.

I watch him walk over to where my mom and grandma are facing off against each other, with my kids in their arms and my family all around them. Wes is holding Anna, and Brooklyn has the baby's twin in her lap. Thank God for this. For them. Thank God this is the legacy I have to give Hope and Ben and any other children who find their way to us.

When I look back, my sister is standing right in front of me with a goofy grin on her face.

"What's that look for?" she asks me.

"I was just thinking how damn lucky we are that this is what we get to give to our kids," I whisper to her. "That this is our legacy."

"Yeah," she whispers. "It's pretty great." And then she adds, "But if you tell them I said that, I'll shoot you in the balls." And then she sack-taps me on her way toward her husband.

"Jesus," I mutter after the breath whooshes out of my lungs, and I gasp a little at the stinging sensation in my junk. "I hate when you fucking do that."

"Language!" my mom and grandma shout at the same time.

"They're babies," I gripe. "They can't talk yet."

"But Seth can," Dad adds, not at all helpfully.

"Seth wouldn't dare repeat that," I say, eyeing my nephew, who is smiling at me with a maniacal grin.

"Wouldn't I though?"

"You better run, squirt." Brooklyn laughs as Seth runs through the house.

"I think we need to make a list," Mama says. "Claire, get a pen and a pad."

"Why me?" my sister whines like she's still eight and not thirty.

"Because I told you to," my mom replies in that way that says she could still catch her and whoop her. I know she is thinking the same thing, because Claire has an unhappy look on her face that says she's remembering the time Mom spanked her in the middle of a church service. The priest never stopped his sermon. Of course, later, we learned he went insane and became a murderer, so I guess the point is moot.

Claire races off to grab one from my office upstairs, when Emma makes her way down. "What's going on here?"

"We came to meet our grandson," Dad says, giving Emma a hug.

"And we figured you needed reinforcements to get all the stuff you need for a second baby," Mom adds.

"And your sister is nosy as fuck," Wes chimes in with a gleeful smile on his face.

"I heard that, you ass!" she shouts from upstairs.

"Aw, baby, you know you love my ass," he retorts.

"Gross, dude, that's still my sister."

"Got it!" Claire says as she comes back into the living room. "What do we need?"

"A crib."

"A double stroller."

"Baby food."

"Size nine months clothes."

"A highchair," I add.

"Toys."

"Oooh, one of those activity jumpers or a walker," Claire inserts. "I bet he'd like that."

"Another dresser."

"Boy blankets and towels."

"And a good jogging stroller," I chime in.

"A second car seat for Emma's car."

"Oooh, better get one for our house too," Dad adds.

"Dad, do you even have room in your car for all these kids?" Claire asks.

"Better stop at the car lot too," he mumbles. "I think I need one of the big vans or an SUV."

"Dad, really?"

"It'll be good for carpooling to Seth's football practices," he says.

"Good idea, honey," Mom agrees, encouraging this baby madness. I just lean back against the wall and look to Wes, who is laughing his ass off. He wasn't born into this kind of crazy family, but he was a fixture in our house growing up, and then when Claire finally made an honest man out of him, he became family legally. He loves every minute of this shit. But then again, I guess I would too if it turned out my parents were murderous psychopaths.

"Should we put a stop to this madness?" I ask him.

"Nah, let them have their fun."

Four hours later, we all left the big box baby store when a huge delivery would be made to our house later tonight, and everyone is now wandering through the neighborhood Target store. I'm pushing a laughing Ben sitting in his new cart cover in the bright-red shopping cart while Emma has Hope strapped to her body. Something my dad fought her for, but seeing as he couldn't figure out the giant sheet of stretchy fabric that she wrapped around her body like origami, she won.

I wrap my arm around her waist and lean into her as she reaches for another box of size three diapers. "You owe me," I rumble in her ear and let myself enjoy the shiver that rumbles up her spine while my lips graze the shell of her ear.

"I know it," she tells me. "I said I did. A deal's a deal."

"No," I whisper. "You owe me. I've spent hours in a baby store, and now I'm in a Target. If you don't sit on my face later and then ride my cock until we both come, I'm going to be seriously disappointed."

"I said, 'a deal's a deal.'" But this time her voice is breathy a la Marilyn Monroe when she sang "Happy Birthday" to President Kennedy, and it has my cock uncomfortably thickening in my jeans. But it doesn't matter, because though I'm still in a Target pushing a shopping cart, I'm now doing it watching my woman bite her lip and squeeze her sexy thighs together when she thinks no one is looking. And I'm doing it all with a shit-eating grin on my face. Life is good.

I pull into the parking lot of the VA clinic, and this time, I'm relaxed. I felt so much better after my first group session that I have no fears of returning. Last time, I was on edge and nervous, but now I know there is nothing to be afraid of.

I pull into a spot, grab my keys, and climb down from my Tahoe. I walk into the clinic and take the elevator to the second floor where Jane's weekly group session meets.

I see Amy as soon as I walk in the room, and I greet him with a smile and a slap on the back man-hug.

"Hey, Ames, how are you?" I ask.

"Oh… uuuh… good, good," he replies, but the look in his eyes say he's anything but.

"You sure about that?" I ask quietly.

"Yeah," he says. "I'm good."

A soft whimper and whine draw my attention to the golden retriever sitting at his feet.

"I'm okay, Chief," Ames says as he pats the dog on the head, and he wags his fluffy tail.

"And who's this?"

"This is Chief, my new service dog."

"That's awesome," I say with a genuine smile. "It's nice to meet you, Chief."

The dog in question holds out his paw for me, and I shake it. He's a beautiful dog. It reminds me that I said one day I'd get the kids a dog. A retriever just like this one. They're supposed to be great with kids. Or maybe a shepherd to herd my growing flock of children. The thought makes me smile.

"What's that look for?" he asks me.

"I was just thinking this past weekend that the kids could benefit from a dog when they're a little bit older."

"Kids?" he asks. "As in plural."

"Yeah." I laugh. "Emma and I had a boy placed with us from Child Protective Services this weekend. He's ours."

"Wow. That's great. Congratulations."

"Thanks."

"Dogs are great," he adds. "Chief is from a program called Purple Paws. They take dogs from shelters in New York and New Jersey and train them for veterans. You can get on a grant list, or you can buy one privately. That's what I did with Chief here."

"I think that's where Ghost got his from, right?" I ask.

"Yeah, his wife is involved with the charity. She's a big animal lover, I hear."

"You got that right. She's got eight cats," I tell him.

"Eight?" He laughs. "I bet Ghost loves that."

"Don't you know it."

"All right," Jane says. "Everyone, grab a seat, and let's get started."

"Think about getting a dog," Ames says. "You won't regret it. He's helped me a lot."

"I will."

"So, who would like to start tonight?" she asks.

"I will," I say.

"Go ahead," she encourages.

"I had a good week, and a bad one," I start. "My wife and I had a child placed with us, and if all goes well, in a few months, we will adopt him. He's a great kid."

"But?" she asks.

"But I am struggling with whether or not I'll be able to protect him or the rest of my family," I explain.

"What makes you think you won't be able to protect them?" Jane asks.

"Just a—" I hesitate to answer. "—a gut feeling."

"Sure," she says. "Let's talk after. I think I have something that might help you."

"Thanks," I say gratefully, because anything would help.

"Would anyone else like to share?"

We all talk about our experiences, our highs and lows for the week, and through it all, Ames looks more and more withdrawn. I watch him through the entire session and notice the large dark circles under his eyes and the pale color to his face. He even looks thinner. Is he eating? Is he sick? I'm worried about him, and after what happened to Palmer, I'm fucking terrified for him.

When the session breaks up, I make my way over to him again.

"You sure you're okay?" I ask him.

"Yeah."

"You can talk to me," I tell him.

"That's rich," he says with a cruel laugh. "We all know this isn't something you're happy about."

"I'm not," I say honestly. "I don't like being here or feeling weak, but I'm doing it because I want to be the man that my family deserves. After what happened to Palmer, I'm worried about you."

"Don't pretend to give a shit," he growls. "You just want to make sure I keep the secrets. Well, I am all right. I'll take them to the grave, so just fuck off already."

And then he stormed out of the room, leaving me surprised at his outburst.

"Everything all right over here?" Jane asks as she makes her way to me.

"Yeah," I reply. "I guess so."

"He'll be okay," she says.

"I hope so," I mumble.

"I want to give you something to try," she tells me.

"This is an oil diffuser with a special blend of essential oils to help promote relaxation and calm. Also, I want you to meet me at my office Thursday for a private session. We'll talk about a medication regimen that will help keep you balanced."

"Okay," I say on a deep exhale. I can do this. "Let's do it."

"Hopefully this helps."

I take the box with the diffuser from her. "I'm going to try it."

I make my way to my car, and as I beep the locks open, I feel both hopeful for my future and worried about Ames's. Could he really mean what he said? I was never the one who forced us to keep the secrets. That was the old CO—I thought. Have I really been holding everyone to his insane orders all this time?

I think about it my whole drive home and am left feeling more unsettled than before. I guess it's possible I'm not remembering things the way they really happened. I feel so confused that I just don't know anymore.

I pull into the driveway and cut the engine. The lights are off in the house, but that doesn't mean Emma isn't still awake and wandering the house. My chest warms at the thought of her and our children here, waiting for me.

There's something about Emma that calls to me like a siren to a sailor. She was made for me and me for her. And there will never be a time that I don't want her. And after our face-off in Target, there's something I want very badly.

I pull my keys from the ignition and head into the house through the garage. The downstairs is dark. I check the back door and the front after closing the garage doors and locking them up tight for the night.

As I make my way upstairs, I realize I left the oil infuser in the car. Shit. I meant to grab it. I'm committed to being the best man I can be for my family, but this doesn't feel like it. This feels like I'm phoning it in, and that's bullshit, so I turn around and make my way back down the stairs and through the garage to my car where it sits next to Emma's.

I grab the diffuser and the vial of blended oils Jane gave me and then head back into the house, this time with my new gadget in my arms and a determination to be a better me. I lock up the garage again and head up the stairs. I set the box on the table at the end of the hall under the big window at the end and check on the babies. Both Ben and Hope are now sleeping in matching cribs. Hope's bedding is pink and floral, and Ben's is all arrows and bucks. Both are in matching footie jammies, with peaceful expressions on their faces as they dance with the stars.

I quietly shut their door and grab my diffuser and oils from the table and carry them through the master bedroom and into the bathroom, where I drop them on the counter. When I turn around and enter the bedroom again, I stop in my tracks, because before where the lights were off and I thought Emma was asleep, now just the lamps on the bedside tables are lit, and she lies back in the center of the bed completely nude with her hand moving between her creamy thighs.

"Getting the party started without me?" I ask.

"Mm-hmm," she moans. "You took too long getting here."

I grab my T-shirt and pull it over my head while I watch her long, slim flingers slip and slide through the wetness between her folds, and I have to taste her. I need it like I need air to breathe. My belt buckle clanks as I shuck my jeans and boxer briefs to the floor. I grip my hard cock in my fist and stroke. I match the tempo of her fingers on her clit and in her pussy. I want us to walk that knife's edge together until I push her over. Only then will I take mine.

I love the way her blue eyes lock on me as she tracks the motion of my hand while I pleasure myself, watching her do the same. When she can't help but let a little whimper slip past her lips, I climb up on the bed and toss her legs over my shoulders. I don't go slow or hold back; I dive in and lick and suck her pussy like I know she needs. She grips the sheets in her hands as I plunge my tongue inside her over and over until I feel her thighs tremble on my shoulders, and she arches her back. I grip her hips tight in my hands and suck her clit hard until she comes.

I don't wait for her to come back down to earth after her climax; instead, I haul her body up the bed so her back is to the headboard and I'm on my knees in front of her. I notch the very tip of me to her opening, and then I slam her down over me. She wraps her arms around my shoulders and tucks her head into my neck as she holds on with everything she has left.

This isn't sweet and gentle, and based on the way I found her when I walked into this room, that isn't what she wanted anyway. My girl wanted a hard and fast fuck, and that's exactly what I'm going to give her.

"Yes," she pants. She's so fucking tight around my cock as I pump up into her waiting body.

"Yeah," I rumble as I move faster and faster and feel her walls flutter over me. "That's it."

"Mm-hmm," she moans as her nails dig into my shoulders.

"Yes. Come on my cock."

The bed creaks as the headboard rocks into the wall behind it. The sounds only serve to drive me higher as I push into her over and over. I couldn't stop if I wanted to. The need to burn up with her is so overwhelming I can do nothing but give in to the feeling that is *liberating*.

And then she's coming so hard on my cock that she's milking me dry, and I can do nothing but drive deep inside her as I follow her over the edge to bliss.

"Welcome home," she says when she catches her breath.

"Glad to be home," I mumble as I slowly slide my cock in and out of her, riding the last tremors of our shared climax. "It's always good to come home to you."

"Mm-hm," she hums.

I lay us both down and cover us with the blankets, and with her wrapped up in my arms; I drift off into a dreamless sleep. And for the first time in a long time, I rest, safely beside her.

Too bad I had no idea it wouldn't last. I guess ignorance really is bliss.

fourteen

the believer

I t's time.

Jonathan Ames is a juicy fruit that is ripe for the picking. I watched him tonight; he's volatile and moody and out of control. He snapped at those around him. No one would be surprised if he took his own life.

But he's not going to take it. I am.

Jonathan Ames needs to pay for his crimes. There is a mountain of sins he needs to atone for, and the time is now. My only regret is that I cannot shout from the rooftops what he has done. He almost said it in last week's group session. I waited and waited and nothing. Not one fucking word about the negligence that cost so many their lives.

Like so many others, he gambled with the devil and

lost. But it was the lives and safety of others he bet on, and it was those people who paid the ultimate price.

I drive through the quiet town. The late-night dark skies provide the cover I need, and only blips of street-lights show sneak peeks of my secrets. Even the moon is a no-show tonight. He must know that only mischief makers are out this late.

I park on a side street and stick to the shadows. It's been a few months since my last act of vengeance, and I've learned from my mistakes. Like how much mess a close-range gunshot wound makes. I won't be doing that again.

I walk around to his house, and the garage door is raised. I walk straight through. I doubt he would lock the door to the house in the state he's in. I know that after a huge fight over his increasingly volatile behavior, his wife and kids are visiting family out of state and won't be back anytime soon. It'll be way too late by the time they come home.

I pull the latex gloves from my pants pocket and slip them on before I try the doorknob, and it turns freely in my hand. I walk into his home and close the door quietly behind me so as not to disturb the neighbors.

The television is on to some twenty-four-hour sports channel. It flips through clip after clip of different games. Jonathan is slumped over on the couch. Liquor and beer bottles litter every surface around him. Every last one of them is empty. There is no way any suspicion would ever arise after the mess he's made of himself. It's too bad; because I enjoyed the merry chase the FBI agent had been on.

He's also on my list, but not yet.

Everything in its due time.

A true believer like me knows to let things happen in the time they're supposed to, even if it's hard to be patient. Waiting was never my strong suit, but after the letdown of the last time, I want to savor every moment I have worked so hard to orchestrate.

The room reeks of stale booze, sweat, and body odor. They go a long way to mask the other scents of the room. Still, none of them should be here if everything was right in Jonathon Ames's world. Will anyone notice what's out of place? Or will I outsmart them again?

The dog yips at me when he sees me.

"Come here, boy," I say quietly and he stands and follows me. I lead him into the washroom off of the kitchen and close the door. He begins to whine and scratch at the door but that's okay, They'll find him soon enough and I can't have him getting in the way of my plans.

"Hi," he says when his red-rimmed eyes flutter open. It's clear he's self-medicating with booze and prescription medication.

"Hi."

"I'm sad," he says.

"I know." I keep my tone soft and soothing. I don't

want to alarm him yet.

"The ghosts won't leave me alone."

"They know what you've done," I tell him.

"They do," he agrees. "I see them everywhere."

"They're watching."

"They see everything," he agrees. "They know everything."

His dog whines in agitation as Jonathon grows more and more emotional. His keening cries will eventually be heard by the neighbors if I'm not careful. I also can't bring myself to kill the dog. I kill monsters, not innocent animals.

"I can make you feel better," I tell him. "You want to feel better, don't you?"

"Yes," he whispers.

"Come on," I say, holding out my hand for him to take it. He does, and I help him to stand and lead him up the stairs.

I could make him forget his pain and feel better one way—with my body—something I've used to get him to let me in his house before. That's where he thinks this is going now, but it's not. His wife knew. I'm sure of it. But still, she never said anything, and if she did, I would deny it.

"I need you to make me forget," he says when we make it to the top of the stairs, and he tries to wrap his arms around me.

"I can't do that," I tell him as I dance out of his

reach.

"I want to forget."

"You can't forget; you have to remember," I say as I slip the loop over his head.

"I don't understand." The look on his face is pathetic. He's so drunk or drugged or both that he can't make sense of what is happening. I'm going to have to spell it out for him.

"You screwed up," I tell him. "You and your team. Innocent people died, because you didn't protect them."

"I didn't tell. I promised not to tell, and I didn't," he panics, but he's too weak to do anything. His dog is crying in the other room.

"And now you have to die."

And then I push him over the banister and watch him hang.

fifteen

from bad to worse

G ray light seeps through the window as the first visages of dawn crawl up from the horizon, and I blink away the last fingers of sleep.

I wonder what woke me up. I was sleeping peacefully. I'm warm and happy cuddled up to my woman, and for the first time in a long fucking time, I did not dream. Whether good or bad, I did not dream. And to be totally honest, I would take a dreamless night over reliving the nightmares of my past mistakes over and over again.

Emma rustles next to me, and I realize something disturbed her as well. One look at the baby monitor shows Hope and Ben are still blissfully in dreamland, and I wonder why I'm not as well.

For someone who hasn't slept well in ages, I'm surprisingly irritated my first night of rest was disturbed before dawn. Or not so surprisingly if you think about it.

Emma rolls out of my arms, grabs her phone from the nightstand on her side of the bed, and swipes her fingers to unlock it before putting it to her ear.

"Dr. Parker," she answers, and I can't wait until it's Goodnite she calls herself by. She's already been talking about taking my name when we get married in a few months' time, and I cannot fucking wait. The thought of her binding herself to me—that we're binding ourselves to each other—so wholly is enough to bring me to my knees and weep in thanks for the rest of my life. I'm so devoted to this woman.

"I'll be right there," she says before hanging up. I'm about to ask her what that was all about when my phone rings as well, and I realize that was what had woken us.

"Captain Goodnite," I answer.

"Captain, this is dispatch," Sally says. She's older and likes the nightshift, because her husband drives a truck and she doesn't like to be home without him. I've known her for years.

"What can I do for you, Sally?"

"Special Agent O'Connell asked me to phone you," she responds. "He's at a crime scene."

"What kind of crime scene?" I ask, but I already know. If Wes is having dispatch phone me, it's not to come out to a tea party before dawn. It's going to be bad and I know it, so I brace, and even though I know what the words coming out of Sally's mouth are going to be before she says them, it's still like a punch to the gut.

"It's a suicide."

"Location?"

"234 Rosebud Avenue."

"I'm on my way," I say before hanging up the phone. I turn to look at Emma and see she's already out of bed and pulling on jeans and my favorite Metallica T-shirt. It's a miracle I'll have any shirts left by the time we're old and gray. At this rate, I'll be naked by Christmas.

"I'll call Dad and see if he can come be with the kids," she says.

"Sounds good."

I pull on jeans and a gray T-shirt. I slide my feet into socks and boots and wind my brown leather belt through the loops with the practice from years of dressing in the dark in the middle of the night. The safe beeps as I pull out my badge and pancake holster that holds my sidearm. I've never carried anything other than a Colt .45, and the feel of it on my belt pulls my focus.

"Hey, Dad," Emma says when he picks up the phone. "Hey, I'm sorry it's so late... or early." She laughs. "Lee and I were both just called to a suicide. Can you come sit with the kids? Do you mind? You're a godsend," she says right before she hangs up.

I grab my drop gun from the safe and tuck it into the holster on my ankle. Not many officers carry a secondary, but life has taught me that you can't be too careful. My dad always carried a secondary, and his dad before him, and I do now, and Claire does too. I know for a fact hers has saved her life more than once, and I never forget it.

"He'll be here in a minute," she says as she pulls her gun from the safe and drops it into her bag. As a medical examiner in our county, she's entitled to carry a weapon, and she does. Emma has always run with the big boys, and I've seen her at the qual range a time or two. I know she takes it and her line of work seriously. "Your mom is staying with the kids there. They aren't up yet… obviously."

"Sounds good," I tell her absentmindedly. There's something about the address that's niggling at the back of my mind, but I'm not fully awake yet to grab on to the information that's still eluding me.

"I love you," she says out of nowhere, and I look at her.

"I love you too."

She tucks her feet into a pair of black Chucks and grabs her bag before we turn down the hallway. We both like to look in on Hope before we leave to see the mayhem and destruction people cause, and now we look to Ben too for that piece of peace and balance.

They're both sleeping soundly. These perfect little bundles of innocence. The world hasn't yet taught them how cruel it can be, and despite how they both entered the world, they have no idea. Somehow, I'll protect them from the dark realities of humanity for as long as I can. I just don't know how.

Emma lets out a heavy sigh, and then I follow her out of their room and down the stairs to the living room just as headlights flash through the dark front windows of the house. My dad is here to look after the kids while we cannot. Building near my childhood home was the best decision I ever made. There's something about this part of town that always feels like home, but now I realize it probably has more to do with the people than anything else. My mom, my dad, even my crazy grandma who has lived with them for years after my grandfather died, and now my niece and nephew. Claire and Wes also built close, and knowing we're all together is a balm on my soul.

Emma doesn't let him knock. She just pulls open the door and gives him a quick hug before handing him the baby monitor.

"I know where everything is," he says, herding us out the door. "The kids are in good hands."

"Thanks, Dad."

"Always."

And then Emma and I climb into my Tahoe and head out. She's already called one of her crew to come with the body mover. I'll lose track of her at the crime scene, as she'll head back to the morgue with the body, but otherwise, we'll meet back up at the station.

We've settled into a nice routine since she became mine and we became an us. We don't hinder each other at work, and I would never put that on her nor she on me. We both know the other carries heavy responsibilities and we each take our duties seriously. But for whatever reason, Emma takes my hand in hers as I drive through our dark neighborhood, and she gives it a reassuring squeeze, only I don't feel reassured at all. I have a feeling in my gut that things are about to go from bad to worse, and there's not one damn thing I can do about it.

And I would soon find out just how right I was.

sixteen

noise complaint

"No," I bite out. "No, no, no, no, no."

"Lee?" Emma asks me, but I'm already out of the car and jogging toward the house. "Lee!"

I knew something was bothering me, but I just couldn't put my finger on what it was. Call it lack of sleep or no coffee firing all my mental cylinders, I don't know, but the minute we pulled up in front of the house of the crime scene, all the puzzle pieces finally fell into place.

This isn't a crime scene; it's a tragedy.

I'm climbing the stone steps in front of the house. Sweat is pouring from my forehead, and my heart is racing in my chest. I feel like I'm going to be sick, and I'm never sick at scenes, not since I was a rookie.

The front door is open as cops mill in and out of the house, and I catch a glimpse, just a second between bodies as they pass in front of someone who saved my life in the desert more times than I can count. They haven't cut him down yet.

"Wes!" Emma screams from somewhere, but I'm not sure where exactly. "He's going down."

I see his feet. I taste bile as it rises up in my throat. I hear a dog whine. And then everything goes black.

"This was a major fuck-up."

Our commanding officer is pissed and rightfully so. This is a shitfuck of epic proportions. Our intel said the terrorist was hiding in the village, but when we got there, they were all dead.

"This op went so far FUBAR it's not remotely repairable," he keeps yelling.

We all stand silent, huddled around him.

"What do you want us to do now?" Ames asks.

"Nothing. Not one fucking thing."

"But—" Donovan starts.

"I said nothing," he growls in Rick's direction.

Ghost shoots him a look to tell him to shut up and back down before he finds his ass in a sling. Our CO is and has always been wound just a little too tight. He's not my favorite SEAL, but the team is where I belong, so I have to put up with his bullshit like everyone else.

"They were all dead when we got there," CO explains—something we all know all too well in a way that the eyes of the dead will haunt me in my sleep. Not only was everyone dead, but also so were my informant and her daughter.

I should have protected them, and I didn't.

And I'm going to have to live with that for the rest of my life. That is if I make it out of the desert in one piece. Donovan seems to be on a one-man suicide mission since his wife left him, and Ghost is determined to take us all with him to protect his crazy ass. But this was more than that.

We made a mistake—a fatal mistake—and it cost hundreds of innocent people, including women and children, their lives.

"So that's what we're sticking with."

"But—" Palmer starts.

"No buts!" CO shouts. "Don't say a word. Don't say a fucking word. Do you understand me?"

"Yes, CO," we all reply.

"Not one fucking word or it'll be your asses in the wind, not mine," he growls, and something burns in my gut. And then he looks right at me, his mean eyes locked on mine, and the words he shares next, I know are meant for me and me alone. And it's also me who will have to carry them with me for the rest of my days. "It's your hands that hold their blood."

"Yes, CO."

"Don't say a word."

"He's coming around," I hear a voice I don't recognize say, and I gasp as I open my eyes and try to sit up all at once.

"Hey there, cupcake," Wes says as he leans over me and slaps my cheek. If I didn't love this guy like a brother, I would seriously kick his ass. Not to mention my head is pounding and I feel like shit right now.

"What happened?"

"You passed out like a rookie," he answers help-fully.

"Awesome."

"Seriously though," he starts. "This is my fault. I should have made sure dispatch told you what you were walking into. That's on me. I'm sorry for that."

"It's okay."

"It's not," he says. "But I'll make it right."

"Okay."

"Ready to get up?" he asks.

"Yeah," I answer.

"Good, because your girl has been clucking over you like a mother hen from the second you hit the ground, and she's making my team nervous."

"That's because she's scary as hell," I tell him.

"I heard that!" Emma snaps.

"That doesn't mean it's not wrong!" Wes laughs.

"You are no longer my favorite brother-in-law."

"I'm your only brother-in-law," he adds helpfully.

"That doesn't mean I like you," she grumbles.

"Yeah, you do," he says before holding out a hand to me. "Up you go, big guy."

"Thanks."

"Think you can handle it?" he asks me.

"Yeah."

Beer and whiskey bottles litter the coffee table, the floor, the sofa, and every other available surface. It's clear Amy was in a bad way and on a bender. I knew he was in a downward slide when I saw him last night, but I thought I could talk to him and everything would be all right. I thought I had time, and once a-fucking-gain, I'm too late. How many men are going to die before I learn my lesson?

"Jesus, what is that smell?" someone asks.

"There's an essential oil diffuser burning in the kitchen," someone else answers, and it reminds me that I have one at home. I wanted to try it out. I was so fucking hopeful, but now I can't help but feel like it's all one big fucking waste, because a lot of good it did Amy.

I look away and see prescription pill bottles overturned and little capsules of all colors and varieties intermingle with the empty bottles.

The house enters into the living room, and the stairs are the backdrop. Thankfully, Amy has now been cut down. Crime scene techs still litter the house, the sounds of cameras snapping evidence photos clicking like crickets in the background. Emma's team has already loaded up Ames to take him to the morgue. The van is gone, but she's still here. She's pretending to supervise the evidence collection, but I know she's just finding busy work to stay close to me. I appreciate it, but at the same time it makes me so fucking mad. I'm not weak, dammit. I'm a goddamn warrior, and I should not be treated like an invalid or a fucking basket case.

I'm not going to jump off the stairs or eat a bullet.

Everyone needs to stand down.

I take a deep breath and try to focus. This place is a mess. Where were his wife and kids?

"Any sign of foul play?" I ask, knowing the only foul play here are the ones perpetrated by my friend on himself.

"No," Wes says quietly.

"I didn't think there would be," I reply. "Where is his family?"

"Neighbor who called in the complaint said he and his wife had a big fight last week, and she packed up the kids and took them to visit family out of state."

"Has she been contacted yet?" I ask.

"Yes. I had a field agent in Alabama make the notification," Wes says.

"I want to know when she comes home," I tell him. "She shouldn't be alone."

"I'll go with you to meet her," he replies.

"What happened here?" I ask.

"Far as I can tell, Amy did what he did, and the dog lost it. Neighbors called in a noise complaint, and the responding officer heard the dog, saw the lights, and no response. He called it in and then entered the premises. Found Amy, and the rest is history," Wes explains.

"What a fucking mess."

"Yeah."

"I just saw him tonight," I mumble.

"How did he seem?"

"I don't know... okay," I say and then change my mind. "Off, I guess. I was going to talk to him about it this week. Now, it's too fucking late."

"Yeah," he replies quietly.

A loud whine and the sound of scratching fill the room. It sounds like the hulk is about to burst through the wood panel door.

"We had to put the dog in the laundry room," Wes says. "Poor pup was freaking out. Won't let any of the women on the team get near him."

"What do you think that means?" I ask.

"I have no idea, but it's fucking weird."

Just then, the latch pops, and the large golden retriever comes barreling in the room and sits down at my feet. He leans his furry body against my legs, tips his head back, and looks at me. His dark-brown eyes are heavy with emotion. His person is gone. I was reading on the Purple Paws website that a lot of service dogs go through a rapid decline of their health after their person dies, and they don't often live much longer. This dog can't be more than a year or two old. It would be a shame if he died because Ames couldn't keep his shit together.

I drop my hand to the top of his head and pet him. He lets out a chuff and leans more of his weight into me. He also doesn't growl or bark like they said he would when Emma approaches me. That's interesting. They made it seem like he hated women. Apparently not my woman though. That's all it takes to make up my mind. The family may want this dog back when they return to their home, or maybe not. I know Ames said Chief was a private purchase, and I will gladly pay the family what they paid for him, but he's mine now. I don't know why—maybe because we both lost a friend tonight, maybe we need each other more than either of us realizes, or maybe it's just because I'm a sucker and he's a great fucking dog. Either way, Chief is mine now.

"Come on, buddy," I say as I pat my thigh and start looking through the house for his doggie paraphernalia.

"What are you doing?" Wes asks.

"Stealing a dog."

"Uhh…" he starts. "I'm not sure that's advised."

"Look," I cut him off. "This dog has been through a lot. He cannot survive on his own for however long it takes Ames's family to get back here and resume his care. I know he was a private purchase, because Ames told me so himself, so he does not have to go back to the organization. And I will gladly write the Ames family a check for him. But he likes me, and I just fucking like him, all right, so I'm taking the damn dog with me."

"Woof," Chief adds.

"See? He agrees with me."

"What about the fact that he doesn't like women?" Wes asks. "You cannot think to bring a violent dog home to your wife and kids."

"Look at him, brother," I reply and look pointedly to the dog in question, who is wagging his fluffy tail and smiling at me with what could only be described as a dopey expression on his face. "Does he look violent to you?"

"Not right this second," he says. "But what about later?"

"Chief," I say to the dog. "Find Emma."

Wes and I watch as the dog stands up, points his nose in the air, and sniffs before trotting over to Emma and sitting down at her feet, smiling his doggie smile at her until she leans down and pets his head.

"Well look at you," she coos. "Aren't you such a sweet boy?"

"Are you sure about this?" Wes asks as he turns back to me.

"One hundred percent," I say with finality. "That dog is mine."

"All right," he relents. "I'll see what I can do to pave the way."

"You have my gratitude."

"You know I'd do anything for you, brother," he says so quietly I know it's for my ears only.

"I know it."

"No half measures."

"I think I'm finally figuring that out," I tell him, but as the words come out of my mouth, I can't help but wonder if they were really true or if they were just another lie I tell myself and everyone else to make us feel better, when in reality it's nothing but a Band-Aid on a snakebite and I haven't sucked the poison out yet.

Maybe some wounds aren't meant to heal, only fester.

And on that thought, I called my new dog to come to me, and he and I walked out into the night. Emma already said she needed to get to the morgue, so she was riding to the station with someone else. I wasn't needed here anymore.

seventeen

the believer

I thought I had more time.

I didn't anticipate the dog causing so many problems. I shouldn't have hesitated to handle the situation. But to me, the dog was an innocent.

I don't hurt innocents.

Only the guilty.

I had no way of knowing he was going to cause such a racket that the neighbors would call the cops. I should have known better. In pretentious suburban neighborhoods like this, the residents are all spying on each other. Now, I just have to pray no one spotted me, or it'll all be over before I can complete my mission.

I regretted my decision to leave the dog behind and decided to rectify it the minute I walked through my front door. I knew I had done wrong and went back *to grab the dog. I wasn't going to hurt him. I'm not a monster. But I could leave him at an animal shelter or pound somewhere far from here.*

I walked right out the door and climbed back in my car, but by the time I made it to his neighborhood, it was crawling with cops, and the blue-and-red lights from their squad cars swirled around the night sky and climbed up the sides of the houses.

I had everything planned down to the minutest detail.

And I messed up anyway.

I'm going to have to fix it, to speed up my timeline, but how? I drive slowly down a side street and watch the cops milling about on the main road, and I know with absolute clarity that Liam Goodnite needs to die.

eighteen

talk to me

"Lee, baby," Emma says as she wraps her body around me, pressing her lush breasts and trim belly into my side.

"Not tonight, honey," I say quietly as I roll to my side away from her.

I didn't look at her face when I rolled away from her. I couldn't. I feel so ashamed. I passed out. What kind of pussy passes out like that? And what does this even mean for my career? I can't be an effective captain and lead my officers if I pass out at a goddamn scene.

And if I can't do my job, then I can't provide for my family. I'm not from money like Wes is, not that he values it other than what it can do. I've always admired my friend for forging his own path and being his own man. He stood up against his parents and all they expected of him, and he lived his life the way he wanted to.

I always knew what path I was on. There was never any doubt in my mind that I was going to be a police officer one day, just as my father had been, and his father before him. I knew I wanted to go into the navy, and I knew I was going to become the man I needed to be to do so there.

The SEALs was a surprise. Once I was in the service, I discovered I was good at it. I learned I enjoyed working toward something and reaching new goals I set for myself. Once in the elite levels of the special ops community, I acquired skills the standard enlistment wouldn't teach me. And I also learned freedoms away from the guilt I felt after spending her entire lifetime avoiding my sister following me and my friends around, wanting to belong with us, even though she was eight years younger. I will never forgive myself for chasing her away that day. I live with the regret that I sent Claire spiraling into the path of the man who would end up taking her from us for five days. And all because I wanted her out of the way for once. It was selfish, and it was stupid, and it almost cost my family immeasurably. Claire paid the heavy price for years without my ever knowing.

That was until I came home and joined the police department. I worked my way up through the ranks, and when Claire was old enough, she again followed in my footsteps. During that time, the FBI had sent Wes all over the country on various cases. We remained close, but it was clear Claire never wanted to hear his name spoken. Something I didn't understand until he came back to George Washington Township and I watched my sister slowly begin to unravel, and I put her in the path of Anna Garner, the department psychiatrist.

Truthfully, it was a selfish plan on my part. I was hoping when she applied to sit the detective's exam, Anna would discover Claire was batshit crazy and I wouldn't have to worry about being able to protect my baby sister anymore, because she would go off and find a nice, safe job. Like as a bank teller. Yeah, right. And pigs could fly. Claire would be more likely to try to reprise the role of old west bank robbers than bank tellers. She'd go on to find a Clyde to her Bonnie, and I didn't realize it at the time, but Wes had seen it too. And he decided to finally quit fucking around and let my sister make an honest man out of him. Claire had other ideas.

I was too busy finding myself in love with my sister's best friend only to discover I had already fucked the third of their trio, and Emma wouldn't give me the time of day because of her duty to her friend. Anna died trying to prove her worth to me when I never should have touched her. I should have set her free to be with someone who appreciated her. Instead, she died, leaving a bigger divide between Emma and me and her blood on my hands. Even if I didn't murder her myself, the one truly responsible is still me.

I had thought after all we had been through, Emma

and I would finally get to live our happily ever after. If anyone was deserving of a fairy tale, it was Emma. I should have known better. I should have never touched her with my soiled hands. I should have let her go when she wanted it. But like always, I ruined it. I ruined everything, because I had to have her. Now, she and Hope, and Ben too, are saddled with a piece of worthless shit like me. What could I possibly give them now? Nothing. That's what.

It's strange that all of this set me on the course for where I am today. That the path I was so surely on, so confident in myself in my youth would lead me to a life to be proud of, would instead be a world of shit I've broken and innocent blood on my hands. And all for what? Not a damn thing.

I should have stayed on the path, but I strayed. I don't know when. It's hard to tell when you're adult life has been one fuck-up after another. But somehow, someway, I didn't just wander off the path; I fell off it completely and thoroughly, and I can't help but feel like there's no going back now.

"Please, Lee," she begs. "You have to talk to me."

"There's nothing to talk about." And there isn't. There really isn't. It's all said and done, another life completely gone, and what to show for it? Nothing. Not one damn thing.

"Lee—" she starts, but I have to stop it. I have to put us both out of our misery.

"It's been a long day," I say quietly but firmly. "Just

get some sleep."

"This was a major fuck-up."

Our commanding officer is pissed and rightfully so. This is a shitfuck of epic proportions. Our intel said the terrorist was hiding in the village, but when we got there, they were all dead.

"This op went so far FUBAR it's not remotely repairable," he keeps yelling.

We all stand silent, huddled around him.

"What do you want us to do now?" Ames asks.

"Nothing. Not one fucking thing."

"But—" Donovan starts.

"I said nothing," he growls in Rick's direction.

Ghost shoots him a look to tell him to shut up and back down before he finds his ass in a sling. Our CO is and has always been wound just a little too tight. He's not my favorite SEAL, but the team is where I belong, so I have to put up with his bullshit like everyone else.

"They were all dead when we got there," CO explains—something we all know all too well in a way that the eyes of the dead will haunt me in my sleep. Not only was everyone dead, but so was my informant and her daughter.

I should have protected them, and I didn't.

And I'm going to have to live with that for the rest

of my life. That is if I make it out of the desert in one piece. Donovan seems to be on a one-man suicide mission since his wife left him, and Ghost is determined to take us all with him to protect his crazy ass. But this was more than that.

We made a mistake—a fatal mistake—and it cost hundreds of innocent people, including women and children, their lives.

"So that's what we're sticking with."

"But—" Palmer starts.

"No buts!" CO shouts. "Don't say a word. Don't say a fucking word. Do you understand me?"

"Yes, CO," we all reply.

"Not one fucking word or it'll be your asses in the wind, not mine," he growls, and something burns in my gut. And then he looks right at me, his mean eyes locked on mine, and the words that he shares next, I know are meant for me and me alone. And it's also me who will have to carry them with me for the rest of my days. "It's your hands that hold their blood."

"Not a fucking chance," I bite out. The bitter taste of dirty orders and defeat sticks to my tongue and clogs my throat.

"I said... don't say a fucking word," he roars as he turns to face off with me, and I swing out, striking his chin with my fist. The men of our team hold me back, which is a good thing, because I probably would have killed him in this moment if I was able, and I fight against them. "That was a mistake."

"Yes, CO," I bite out. "So was trusting you. I won't make that mistake again."

"Don't say a word."

"Got it."

"Oh shit," someone gasps, and I quit my thrashing.

I blink the last of the dream away and reach for the lamp on the bedside table. I flip the switch, and half of the room fills with soft light. Just at the edge of it, where it begins to blur back into the darkness of the middle of the night, I see Emma hunched over, clutching her cheek.

"Emma?" I ask, and the burning in my gut intensifies.

"It's fine," she says. "Really. It was my fault."

"What was?" I ask, and I know without a doubt I do not want to know whatever it is she thinks is her fault. And I also know without a doubt that I have to know, because there is no way it was her fault; it was all fucking me.

"It's no big deal," she says, and when she does, she turns her head just enough that I can see through a slash of light what happened. What has been done.

"No." I don't even realize I've spoken, that I called out, cried, because I am so overcome with the knowledge that I struck her. My Emma, my partner, the woman I love so fiercely, the woman I fought so hard for. I've hit her, struck her, marred her beautiful face, and there is no coming back from that. "I'm so sorry."

"Lee, it's not your fault," she says. "You were dreaming, and I tried to wake you. You've told me time and time again not to try to wake you, and I did. I knew better. It's my fault."

"No, it's fucking not."

"Really, Lee," she says. "It's no big deal."

"It is a big deal!" I shout. "Do not say it's not a big deal, because it fucking is."

"Okay," she says.

She holds her hands up to placate me, and it might have worked. I feel myself softening toward her, but then one of the babies cries, and my crimes are compounded. I've upset them all. I've harmed their mother. What next? Killing the dog? All I know is I cannot be here a minute longer.

"I have to go."

"No!" she cries. "No, Lee. You can't leave me like this."

"Don't you see what I've done?" I shout. "I've hurt you. I can't hurt you."

"Your leaving is hurting me!" she cries. Emma tries to grab me, but I evade her hands. I don't know how, because I'm terrified to hurt her again. I have to go.

"I have to go," I say again. "I have to think."

"Think here."

"It's not safe. You're not safe if I do."

"I don't care," she cries. "I just want to be with you!"

"I want to be with you, but right now, I can't. I don't trust myself."

"Please," she pleads, and the sound of her voice tears my heart in two. But I have to go. There's no way around it.

I quickly pull on jeans and a T-shirt. I stuff my feet in my running shoes and pull a hoodie over my head. I grab my gun and badge from the safe and tuck them into my pockets with my wallet and phone. I grab a small duffel from the closet and toss some clothes in it, my toothbrush, and razor. Anything I can get my hands on, really.

"Where are you going?" she asks.

"I don't know yet."

Ben adds his wails to Hope and Emma's, and it's more than I can take. I whistle, and Chief comes running. "Come on, boy."

"Lee, please," she begs. Her voice is desperate, and I hate I've put it there. She should be nothing but happy and carefree. "Don't go. Don't do this."

"I have to."

I don't want to look at her. I know that if I do, I won't want to go. I already don't, but I know it's the right thing to do. She's beautiful; then again, she always is. Her blue eyes are red-rimmed, and tears course down her pink cheeks. But it's the harsh purple color and swelling coming up on her jawline that I needed to see to know I have no place in this home with her or these innocent children. I'm not a warrior anymore. I've become a monster.

And with that thought, I turn and leave the house I built with her in mind to raise our family in. I'll make sure she has it for as long as she wants it. I climb into my Tahoe after Chief jumps in, and I pull out into the night. I drive to the next town over, the one where the VA clinic is, and find a motel. I don't need fancy. I just need a place to shower and sleep—that is, if I ever can again. Emma's bruised and tear-stained face will no doubt be added to the visions of ghosts of my past mistakes that haunt me at night when I close my eyes.

I check into the room and have to pay a pet deposit on Chief, but it's worth the extra fifty bucks. Now more than ever, I can't let him go. I need him. I know it in my gut. I just don't know how. I unlock the room and let us in. He immediately claims the bed that is far smaller than the queen-sized bed the clerk downstairs claimed it to be.

The room smells of stale whiskey and old cigarettes, but I don't care. I strip off my clothes and climb under the scratchy sheets and let my dead friend's service dog spoon me. Really, he wouldn't have it any other way. I thought sleep would finally claim me, but like always, I'm wrong.

nineteen

help

I need help.

I didn't sleep all night. I laid there in the terrible motel room bed with its scratchy sheets, unable to close my eyes, because every time I did, I saw Emma huddled on the floor, holding her cheek, and knowing it was me who put her there. I hate it. I hate everything about it.

It makes me sick to my stomach. I love her so much. She's smart, and she's sweet, and she can be so fucking funny, and I hurt her. I put her on the floor, holding her cheek, and I can't unsee it. I can't undo it, and I have the sinking feeling in my gut that I can't move on either.

So I left. I left the only woman I have ever loved, because I put her on the floor with a bruise marring her beautiful face. So I couldn't sleep. I didn't even try.

Not to mention, Chief hogs the bed.

This morning, I got up and showered in a stall that was too small and too short for a man my size. I had to duck to get my head under the lukewarm spray. Overall, the whole thing made me edgy and cranky.

I dressed in the limited clothing supply I had with me, grabbed my sidearm and my badge, and hooked both to my belt. I slung my worn leather jacket up my arms, jumped in my Tahoe with Chief, and drove to the station, where I drank the shit coffee from the kitchenette and hid in my office like the goddamn pussy I am from my woman who works in the same station. I'm in too deep, and I don't know what to do.

I don't even know if she's here or if she called in sick. Would she come to work and let everyone here get a good look at her? Would she tell them it was me who struck her in the middle of the night? No one has said anything to me; in fact, no one has even come into my office. All are hiding from the beast I seem to be today, choosing instead to email in their updates and reports. I can't say I blame them either. I wouldn't want to be near me.

I reach for the cup of coffee on my desk that went cold hours ago, but I can't bring myself to leave the safety of my office, so I'll drink it anyway. The door swings open without anyone knocking or announcing their arrival. It has me on edge and my anxiety spiking through my body. Chief whines. And even though it's only been two seconds since the door swung open, it slams again, only this time with an angry Wes standing inside my sanctuary.

No, I was wrong. He's not angry; he's furious.

"What the fuck is going on?" he roars.

"What?" I ask quietly. Almost too quietly to be heard.

"You want to try again, brother?" he bites out. "And try real fucking hard when I ask you what the actual fuck is going on."

"It was an accident," I tell him. "I'm fixing it."

"Brother, you are not fixing jack shit."

"She's safe now," I whisper, and I know from the look on his face that he can hear how broken I sound, which incidentally is just the tip of the iceberg of how broken I actually am. "I'm away from her. She'll be safe now."

Wes just stares at me for a long time, and I must have misplaced my crystal ball, because I have no fucking idea what he's thinking. Thankfully, he decides to lay it on me.

"You cannot be this much of a fucking moron," he says.

"Excuse me?" I bark. "I'm trying to do the right fucking thing here."

"Well, you're doing it fucking wrong," he roars.

"You do not know that!"

"I do, seeing as how I'm not talking about the big-ass fucking bruise on her face," he says. "I'm talking about the fact that she's down there in that creepy as fuck basement morgue of hers, crying her eyes out to your fucking sister about how you do not love her anymore. And your sister, who just so happens to be my wife, is pissed. And when I say pissed, I mean you better fix it, and you better fix it fucking fast, or else you better have a passport in an assumed name and plane tickets to the jungles of Nicaragua, because she's mad as hell, and we're all going to pay for your crimes if you don't man the fuck up and fix your relationship. So man. The fuck. Up."

"I can't," I say quietly.

"You can, and I hope to God you pull your fucking head out of your ass and fix your shit," he says.

"I will," I say, but as soon as I do, I'm not entirely sure it's true. In fact, I'm pretty sure it's a lie, and we both know it.

"Get help."

"I will."

"And call your fucking shrink and fix this mess," he says. "Before you fuck up the best thing to ever fucking happen to you."

And then he storms out of my office, slamming the door behind him as he goes. I lift the cup of cold coffee to my lips and drink it, because… well, what else am I going to do? Everything else is a goddamn mess.

Tick... tick... tick...

The clock on the wall reminds me that every second that ticks by is one I am colossally fucking up. And I know I am. I just don't know how to stop it. There is no way to please everyone.

I know Wes and Claire and even Emma think I should just go back home and live my life, but at what cost? They don't know. They don't understand. There are demons that live deep inside me, and I can't get them out. They can't be exorcised.

I want more than anything to be able to go home and be with my family. I love them, and I miss them, and it's killing me every day—every single second of every day—not to be with them. But if I hurt one of them... I couldn't live with myself.

There's a quiet voice in the back of my mind that whispers, *Is this really living? Would I be okay living like this, alone, and apart from my family?* I just don't know. I guess I need to take it one day at a time, because right now, I can't stop seeing Emma clutching her cheek. Or worse, the bruise that mark up her gorgeous face.

If it were anyone else who hurt her, I would kill them, and I wouldn't even bat an eye, so why should it be any different when I'm the one who caused her harm?

The clock finally strikes five—quitting time, in theory—and I can cut out for the day. Emma will be on her way to collect the kids from my mom and dad's, and then she'll be spending the evening making dinner for her and Ben, giving bottles and baths, telling bedtime stories, and tucking them in. And she will be doing it all without me.

But then again, I guess time marches on.

Emma and I are not married. There's nothing stopping her from moving on one day. Will she? My gut burns at the thought of her with another man. She's mine, and she always will be. But will she feel that way now that I'm not at home?

No. I can't think like that. If Emma moves on to someone better, then I should be happy for her. I should let her move on and find the happiness I can't give her anymore, because I love her that much.

I pull my gun and my badge out of my desk drawer and clip them to my belt as I push back from my desk and stand. Everything is locked down, my computer turned off for the night, and I have somewhere I need to be, even though it's going to suck.

I grab my jacket from the door and slip it up my arms. I pop my head out of my office door and look down the hallway both ways to see if anyone is coming. It's absolutely ridiculous and I know it, but today has been a shit day, and I just don't want to make it any worse. I know Emma should have left long ago, but still, I'm not ready to see her. I'm not ready for her to see me like this. I feel weak and vulnerable, and I don't like it. I should be her protector, and now they all need protection from me.

The coast is clear, so I leave my office with Chief, locking the door behind us, and make my way down the hall to the back parking lot. My Tahoe is parked toward the back, and I climb in and head toward the VA Clinic.

I've felt like the world was lifted off my shoulders after every group session, but now, who knows. Chief barks from his seat next to me, reminding me I'm not totally alone.

Maybe things will get better. Then again, maybe they won't. I can't help but feel like nothing is ever going to be the same again.

twenty

killing me

I'm struggling to grasp the calmness, the relief that I normally feel when I'm outside of the VA Clinic, but tonight, there's nothing there. Absolutely nothing.

Just… nothing.

I suck in a deep breath and force it back out. I do it again and again. And… no change. Well, at least I tried. I look to Chief, his big brown eyes burrowing into my soul. I wonder if he thinks Ames is going to be here for him, or if he knows that he's gone. I heard service dogs don't last much longer than their service members, but at the same time, he seems to have attached himself to me. I just don't know. What I do know is that after only seventy-two hours, I couldn't bear to be parted from him. I couldn't cope if he died right now.

"Ready?" I ask him before I get out of the car. My badge and gun are already stowed in the glove box and locked up safely.

"Woof."

We walk into the clinic, and my gut burns and my heart clenches. This is for people who can be fixed, people who don't carry the demons that I do. Like Ames did. Maybe we don't get to be saved.

Maybe we don't deserve it.

I feel edgy and agitated. It's almost like my skin is on too tight. Whether Chief feels my emotions or he's having his own moment, I don't know. All I know is that he's chuffing beside me. It's not quite a whine, but I can tell he's unsettled at the very least.

There's a smaller crowd here tonight. Not many people. And those who are here are just now finding out in real time what happened to Ames, that Amy, who was one of us in every way—a soldier, a veteran, a husband and father, and a man who was suffering his demons—had lost the fight. Gone too soon. And everyone in this room knows that at some point in time, we've craved the bite of the bullet or begged for peace and mercy to come one night in our sleep. But there is no peace to be had. There is no mercy to be found. Maybe we're all just dead men walking. Maybe one by one, we'll all realize it's time to give up the ghost, or really that it's time to lay down our swords and our shields and let the ghosts win, because in the end, they always do.

Jane is there, looking somber. I feel bad. I know she believed in Amy, that she believed in all of us, and I can see by the way she's holding herself that this defeat is a low blow to her. She did not want to lose him.

When I finally called Ames and asked him about the program that he was in at the VA, he spoke about Jane and her work with him and the other men in the group at length. He felt Jane was the secret to his success and that, without her, he would have been dead a long time ago. He told me that he felt like he was slowly dying, slowly turning into someone else, something he didn't know how to be or how to live with, but Jane gave him back himself. I was so hopeful talking to him. I thought that if I just did what she told me to, used the oil diffuser, took the meds, and came to group therapy, that I could get my life back on track, that I could be the man Emma and our kids need me to be. But now I can't help but feel like that man died in the small Afghan village twenty years ago.

I walk over to the table at the back of the room and fix myself a cup of coffee. I don't need more caffeine with how anxious I already feel, but the lack of sleep is also getting to me. Not to mention, a hot cup of something to hold in my hands might make me feel a little more grounded on a night when I can't help but feel like I'm slipping away, like everything is spinning out of control.

"When everyone's ready," Jane says, "let's all take our seats."

I make my way over to one of the folding chairs in

the circle and sit down. Last time I was here, I watched Amy and knew something was off with him. I should have spoken to him about it. I should have pushed when he said he was fine. He wasn't fucking fine. He knew it; I knew it. We all should have done something about it. I didn't, and now it's just too fucking late.

"Before we begin," Jane says as the last people milling about take their seats. "I want to let you all know that last night, Jonathan Ames took his own life."

Even though I knew it was coming, it's like a punch to the gut. I hate it. Amy should be here now, telling us all to nut up and get on with the mission, get on with our lives. But he's not, and now I'm not sure if I can keep going. It feels like every time I take one step forward, it's followed by three steps back. I've lost my friends, my family, and at some point in time, I'm going to lose my job. This is not healthy. And to be totally honest, I'm not sure my judgment isn't impaired right now.

I just don't trust myself anymore.

"Now that that's out of the way," she says, and I hate the words. Ames isn't out of the way; he's dead. He's fucking dead, and he was part of this group for a lot longer than I was, and it feels wrong that she used those words. "Let us begin."

No one says anything. We all look to our boots. Chief barks a high-pitched bark, and I put a hand to his ruff between his shoulder blades and whisper to him quietly. He still seems agitated, but he settles down some.

Still, no one talks.

"How about you, Lee?" Jane prompts as she turns to me. "Why don't you start us off?"

Fuck. Fine. I guess I'll begin. "I'm not okay," I start.

"How are you not okay?" she asks me. I look around the circle and see eyes on me. They aren't un-friendly, just... wary. We all know we're not okay; oth-erwise, why would we even be here? If I was doing all right, I'd be home with my woman and our kids, not in this clinic waxing poetic about all the ways I've fucked up my life.

"Last night was not good," I answer. "Although I have been a constant not good for a while, last night was bad."

"What happened last night to change things?"

"Last night, I was called to the scene of what I thought would be a crime," I answer. "It turned out to be Ames. W-w-when I saw him, I lost it. I blacked out. I haven't been like that since I was a rookie. I don't black out at scenes. I don't have panic attacks."

"Perhaps we can work out some meditation tech-niques that will help you in the future," she says, and I wonder what kind of future a police officer could have that has panic attacks at a death scene.

"That's not all that happened last night," I say qui-etly, but now I'm in for a penny, in for a pound. I have to get it all out. It's like vomit; I can't choke it back. I won't feel better until it's all out of my body, out of my mouth.

"What else happened?"

"Afterward, we were home, and I was asleep," I start to explain. "In bed with my girl. I was having a dream—"

"Do you dream often?" she interrupts to ask me.

"Yes," I bite out as if the admission has to be ripped from me. It's not something I'm proud of. In fact, I hate it; I hate to feel so weak.

"And what was the dream about?" she asks. She seems almost… I don't know, excited. Maybe it's that I'm making a breakthrough where before I had just been coasting, but she looks like she really wants to know. Maybe if I can get through this, I'll be okay after all.

"I can't say," I explain. "It was something that happened overseas."

"I understand," Jane says while the other men nod. We all dream about the stuff we can't leave behind, the people who didn't make it back home, and missions that went so far beyond fucked up that anyone was lucky if they made it home in any form other than in a flag-covered pine box. "Do you have this dream often?" she asks, and the question seems innocuous enough, but to me, the truth is the final nail in my coffin.

"All the time," I whisper.

"And what do you do when you have this dream?"

she asks.

"I don't know. It depends on how bad it was at the time. Sometimes, I get up. Sometimes, I throw up. Sometimes, I might go for a run, or sometimes, I might fuck my girl," I admit with a smirk that makes the other guys smile or chuckle.

"The long-time regulars will tell you that while physical activity is not a bad thing," she says with a fair amount of censure in her voice, "sex is not the answer."

"It felt like it at the time," I mutter, making the guys laugh some more.

"And do you feel better after, when you do?"

"Sometimes."

"But not this time?" she asks.

"No," I answer quietly. "Not this time."

"What happened last night?" she questions. "When you had your dream?"

I take a deep breath and then let the words flow out of me. My admission makes me sick to my stomach. I want to run, to hide. I want to pretend like it didn't happen, but that's not who I am. So I let it all out.

"Last night, I was having the dream again," I start. "But when I didn't wake up, my fiancée tried to wake me. Instead of waking up, when she touched me, I hit her."

"Is she all right?" someone asks.

"Yeah," I answer. "In the sense that she will be

okay. She's bruised and scared."

"What did you do?" Jane asks.

"I took one look at her holding her cheek and knew what happened, what I had done, so I told her that I can't be there. I can't hurt her or one of the kids. I would die. I couldn't live with myself if…." I trail off. I can't even voice what I'm feeling right now.

"I get that," she says. "Are you using the diffuser?"

I wonder what's going on with the diffuser that could possibly help when I'm this far gone.

"A little," I admit. "I just don't know what it could do to help at this point. Everything just feels like it's too far gone, that I'll never be able to put my life back together."

"And how does that make you feel?" she asks.

"Weak," I answer. "It makes me feel like a failure, like I have failed everyone and that there is no hope."

"I'm going to write you a new prescription after the meeting," she says. "Let's not give up hope just yet. All right?"

"All right."

The rest of the meeting goes quickly. More share the same. They're struggling to make it day to day, but overall, no one seems as fucked up as me, although everyone is feeling the loss of Ames. It makes me wonder if I even belong here. These men still have hope. They're struggling but then get it together every day, while I'm spiraling out of control. I was a goddamn

Navy SEAL, and now I'm a goddamn police captain. I should make chief one day, not wash out like I'm about to. It's pathetic. It's embarrassing.

When the meeting wraps up, I take the script Jane wrote for me to the all-night pharmacy and fill it before heading back to my sad and lonely motel room. I might as well try it tonight and see if I can't catch some sleep.

I eat a burger from a drive-thru place and put down some kibble for Chief. We catch the tail-end of a game on TV, but I'm not really listening. Something about that player from Texas setting a record. Who knows?

I take Chief out for one last walk and then climb the rickety metal motel stairs up to my room. The sky is clouding over, and even though it's late, I can tell a storm is moving in. I can smell it in the air.

I strip out of my clothes and run a chipped glass under the faucet, filling it with lukewarm water. I pop open the bottles and toss back a bunch of pills before washing them down with the water. I have never been a big pill taker. I hate it. And I have never wanted to become dependent on one substance over another. Booze and pills were never going to be vices of mine. And I've seen one too many good men and women go down like that. It's just not worth it. But I also can't go forever without sleep. I need rest so I won't become a danger to myself and those around me. So I'll try it and hope for the best. If not, then I won't do it again.

I finish the glass and then set it on the edge of the sink before lying down in the scratchy sheets and praying that sleep claims me. Or death. Whatever. Beggars can't be choosers and all that shit.

twenty-one

true believer

It's almost time.

I could hardly believe it when he said he was having nightmares, that he's acting violently. And all without my help. I couldn't be happier that things are progressing so quickly.

I would have thought that Goodnite, being so solid in his life and career with his family around him and his fiancée beside him, wouldn't fall to the demons, but it just goes to show what a guilty conscience will do to you. He is guilty of so much, and the blood of many stains his hands.

I know exactly why he doesn't sleep at night.

If I keep to this schedule, I can find a way to get to the FBI agent and then maybe even the president and his man. Although, I think I might have to wait to get *them until they are no longer in the White House. When Chancellor and Donovan take their families back to New York, then I'll strike. With another incarnation of terror they won't see coming.*

I suppose I should feel sad that things are progressing so rapidly. That I haven't had time to play with him like I hoped I would. Like a cat with a mouse, but this mouse is a wily one. He's isolated from his family, and now is the time to strike.

I can't go to him tonight, because it's too soon after Jonathon Ames, but I also can't wait too long. I can't risk him going back to his family or finding out who I really am either. It was a close one with the dog. I was worried for a minute that the mutt would out me for the killer I really am. And it was a lucky break that Goodnite didn't put two and two together. I should have done something about the dog last night, but now it goes to show that I can't. He's out of my reach... for now. But then again, no one is out of my reach now.

A true believer is always on the righteous path, and tonight, that path is vengeance.

twenty-two

come home to me

Eyes.

The smell of sulfur fills my nostrils, and smoke sears my lungs. The heavy weight of the rifle in my hands is like second nature to me. I could carry it in my sleep. During training, I probably did.

But it's the eyes that chill me to the bone in the middle of this hot desert.

I don't know how the intel had gone so bad. I know it happens, but not like this. One minute, the mission was going to plan, and the next, the world exploded. Spurts of gunfire can be heard all around me, but it's the screams that ring in my ears.

"Fuck, fuck, fuck," I hear Adams scream through the comm in my ear. "They're dead. They're all dead."

And he's right. They're all dead. Every last one of

them. I was helpless to prevent this, and still I feel like I should have. It's as bad as if their blood was directly on my hands.

I make my way through the village we've been watching, my heart in my throat. Buildings, homes, the carts in the market, they're all gone, burned-out shells of what they were before. And bodies crumpled where they fell. Men, women, children, death does not discriminate. Their eyes vacant after life left them.

If eyes are the window to the soul, then this is a portal to hell as I look at the faces of each person who should not have died. A child we gave a candy bar to yesterday, an old woman who offered coffee in the market, and a beautiful young woman whose belly was swollen with a baby.

Her dark eyes watch me, haunt me, as she sees me and nothing at all. And then they change to the green of Emma's, her belly cut open and our child just gone. I was helpless to stop it. I should have known what would happen. I should have protected them, but I didn't.

The smoke burns my throat as I turn to the left and see Emma's blonde-and-pink hair, her green eyes open and watching me, her beautiful body mutilated, because I was in her life.

"No!" I shout.

But the eyes of the dead scream that this is all my fault.

"No!" I gasp as I come awake.

I'm not sure what woke me up. The pills have me feeling out of sorts and groggy, almost like I'm treading through quicksand. But the dream has me gasping for breath while my heart feels like it's going to beat out of my chest, and sweat rolls down my back.

There's a knock at the door.

"Lee, honey, open the door," Emma calls out. "Please."

I toss the scratchy covers back and stand up. I'm heading for the door before I realize I shouldn't. If I let her in, I won't be able to stay away, because the memories of Emma bleeding out on our living room floor, her beautiful pregnant belly cut open like a gruesome smile, it all reminds me of how close I had come to losing Emma and Hope, how close I came to losing it all.

"Please, honey," she calls softly, and like a moth to a flame, I can't stay away.

I pull open the door and see her strawberry hair is pulled up on top of her head, but the bits and pieces that usually fall out and float around her face are stuck to her head haphazardly with rainwater. She's in a pair of leggings and one of my sweatshirts. Her feet are tucked into her black Chucks, and I'd be surprised if I saw her wearing anything else.

She's a mess, but she's also the most beautiful thing I've ever seen.

"What are you doing here?" I ask.

"I had to see you," she says. "Can I come in?"

I know I shouldn't. I know that if I push open the door and let her in, I won't be able to turn her away. I won't be able to keep her at an arm's length, even if it's for her own protection. I don't know what to do.

So I push open the door.

Emma ducks under my arm as she moves quickly around me and into the motel room. I let the door shut and turn back to her. She looks wrong in this shitty place. She should never be here; someone like Emma should have the best of everything, even if that best is not me.

"I miss you," she says, and the pills I took still have me in a fog. I feel like I can't think clearly. "Please, Lee. I can't stay away."

She steps closer to me and wraps her arms around my waist. She presses the front of her body to mine as she pushes up on her toes and touches her mouth to mine.

It's a reflex. It's almost like second nature; in fact, it is as natural as breathing to me to lean into her and deepen the kiss. I lick into her mouth hungrily as the memory of how I could have lost her flashes behind my eyelids. Emma's bright light was almost extinguished, and now I want nothing more than to bathe in it and let it fill me up. It might not be the right thing to do, but in this moment, I don't give a fuck.

I grab the hem of my sweatshirt and pull it up over her head with the tank she had on underneath it and nothing else. Her full breasts swing free as I toss the discarded clothing aside, and I watch her pink nipples tighten.

She arches into me, and my hard cock presses against her lower belly when it tents my shorts. I walk her backward toward the bed Chief vacates with a half-hearted grunt before he collapses on the floor to resume his beauty sleep.

I toss her onto the bed, and she bounces. I grab the waistband of her leggings and pull them down, exposing her bare pussy to me. It's pink and plump, and it glistens for me. I love that she wants me so badly, even though it rips me apart as well.

I strip the material down her legs, flinging her sneakers off where they fall, and toss them to the ground before dropping to my knees beside the bed. I throw her legs over my shoulder, because I'm suddenly starving. I need to taste her, to fuck her with my mouth, to know she's here and she's alive. I need it like I need air to breathe.

I don't start easy as I grip her thighs. I dive right in, licking her, sucking her lips into my mouth, and nipping her there. I plunge my tongue deep inside and pull on her clit. I work her, eat her, licking and biting and sucking. I *devour* her, and I can't get enough.

She digs her heels into my back, and her fingers tangle in my hair as she pulls me to her. My girl can't get enough of my tongue, of my mouth. She likes it when I fuck her with everything I've got, and she wants to come; that's clear enough to understand, but not yet. I'm not ready to let her have what she wants just yet.

I stand up from the floor, and when I pull away from her, she lets out a small mewl of protest, but she also knows I won't leave her hanging for long. I push my shorts to the floor, and my hard cock springs free. I crawl over her body and kiss her, licking into her mouth, letting her taste herself on my tongue so she knows how much I want her and how much she wants me.

But just as I settle over her, Emma digs a heel into the bed and rolls, pushing me to my back and her on top. It would seem that my kitten is in the mood to play tonight, and I have a mind to let her... *for now*.

I lie back and watch as she slithers down my body and grabs my cock in her fist. She doesn't keep me waiting long as to what she's going to do with it. She pumps it in her hand once... twice... and then I get the view of a lifetime as she wraps her full pink lips around the tip.

I could watch her all night as she licks up my shaft before swirling her mouth around me over and over. I open my legs wider so she can settle between them as she pumps my cock, twisting her fist around it.

She twirls her mouth around the tip again before settling into a steady rhythm as she bobs over my shaft. I groan as she slides up and down my length and lay my heavy palm on the back of her head to guide her up and down, faster and faster, as she works my cock with her pretty pink mouth.

But I don't want to come in her mouth. If I'm going to let myself give in to the fantasy of Emma, then I want it all. I want her pussy.

I grab her bun in my fist and pull her up and off my cock. Her green eyes take in the expression on my face, and I can see the questions in their depths, but she knows me, and she knows what I want. I watch as her body flushes pink with her banked arousal. I didn't let her come before, but now I'm going to, and she knows it.

She crawls back up my body and straddles my hips. She rocks back and forth over my hard length, and the slippery heat of her moving over my shaft has my balls drawing tight and me clenching my teeth.

Finally, she settles over the very tip of me and slides down.

She braces her hands on my shoulders, and then she starts to move. Rocking back and forth, she undulates her hips, sliding me in and out of her heat. In slow, fluid movements, she works my cock, and I glide my hands up and down her sides, her back, over her ass, and back up her sides again, only to repeat the path over and over.

I pluck a nipple between my thumb and index finger, making her moan and grind down over me. And I want to do it again to see if I can make her lose her focus, if can I make her come, but she leans over me and presses her mouth to mine. I take the opportunity to lick into her mouth while I grab her by the hips and thrust up into her from below.

"Yes," she pants against my lips, and I thrust up

again, harder this time.

But still, she pushes back up so she's hovering over me and holds onto my shoulders tight while she rides me. She pulls up, keeping only the very tip of me inside her before she slams back down, impaling herself on my cock. She rises up and slams down again and again.

"Yes," she cries as she fucks herself on my cock, and it's the sexiest thing I have ever seen.

"Yeah," I growl. "That's it. That's it."

I grip her hips tight in my hands as she moves faster and faster, her race to the finish line nearing, and I can see it move over her face as her movements become less fluid and more erratic.

"That's it, baby," I rumble.

"Lee," she pleads.

"Let it go," I tell her. "Give it to me."

"Yes."

She drives herself down on my cock as she drops to her elbows. Her hands are still holding onto my shoulders, and her full breasts are pressed to my chest as she grips my shaft in her tightness, and wave after wave of her climax ripple over me.

I take over where she left off and hold her hips tight as I drive up into her from below. Faster and faster, I pound into her, and her beautiful mouth drops open over my collarbone as she screams her way through her climax.

It doesn't take long after her for me to find mine, and I thrust up once... twice... three times more before I plant myself deep inside her and follow her over the edge with my arms wrapped tight around her slim body and her face tucked into the side of my neck.

My breath saws in and out of my lungs, and I hold her tight like I never want to let go as I struggle to get my heart to beat right, because here she is in my arms, alive and breathing and fucking mine. My cock is still deep inside her, joined in the most primal of ways, making the memories of how I almost lost her fade, because here she is.

And then she tips her head back, and whispers, "I missed you, baby." And it's like a bucket of cold water was thrown over my head.

I can't have her. I can't have this, because if I let my guard down, even a little bit, Emma could get hurt, or worse. And if something happened to her because of me, I couldn't go on. I can't live in a world where I'm the monster who hurts her. I just can't.

"Hop up," I say quietly, leaving no doubt that I need her to move, because the fun and games are over.

"Lee?" She sounds scared, hesitant, and I hate that I put that there in her voice.

"Hop up," I say again, this time firmer, and I roll to the side, taking her with me when she doesn't move. I slip from her body, hating every minute she's no longer connected to me, her body no longer one with mine.

I throw my legs over the side of the bed, and Chief

whimpers but also stays where he is, lying on the floor with his head resting on his paws and his eyes watchful. I rest my forearms on my thighs and drop my head into my hands. My head is pounding, and my heart is breaking.

"Lee?" she calls again.

"I think you need to go," I say quietly, my voice as dead as my heart.

"No," she says firmly. "I won't."

"Just go."

"No, Lee. Come back to me," she pleads. "I had you for a moment, and now you're trying to pull away from me again, and I don't want it. I won't allow it. Come home to me."

"You won't allow it?" I ask, and I'm pissed. I'm so mad. Can't she see this is killing me?

"No, I won't allow it," she says. "Come home to me."

"Can't you see this is killing me?" I shout aloud.

"I had you for a minute," she repeats. "Come back to me."

"You had my cock," I say cruelly. "I want you; that's no secret, and it's also not a far stretch of the imagination to think that I always will."

"Lee—"

"You suck my cock and ride it like a pro, but that doesn't negate the fact that this was a mistake," I say.

"Don't say that," she whimpers, and I can hear the tears in her voice, but I don't look back at her to confirm their presence. "I love you."

"And I love you."

"Then come home to me," she pleads. "Why are you doing this?"

"I'm trying to fucking protect you!" I roar. "Don't you get it? You're not safe with me."

"You would never hurt me," she says, and I laugh cruelly.

"We both know that's a lie," I say coldly. "All you have to do is look in a mirror to know otherwise."

"That was an accident—" she starts, but I cut her off.

"Don't even bother to try and lie to me," I tell her. "We both know it's a waste of your breath."

"Don't say that!" she cries. "You are not a waste!"

"I'm a lot of things, honey," I reply. "And a waste is number one on the list. I need you to get your things and leave."

"Lee," she pleads. Her tone of voice is desperate and so unbearably sad. I have to cut this off while we're both still standing, even if my heart feels like it's nothing but an open wound and every second in her presence does nothing but make it bleed.

"And don't come back."

I stand up from the bed, grab my shorts, and head into the bathroom, locking the door behind me. I flip the knobs on the shower and open up the taps. Maybe I'll feel better if I can just get clean, but I can't help but feel like I'll never be clean again.

I take my time, soaping up my body and washing my hair. I turn off the taps and grab one of the bristly towels from the rack and dry off before pulling my shorts back on. I nervously pull open the bathroom door, not sure what I'm hoping to see or not see when I do. I know that the chickenshit in me wants her to be gone so I don't have to face another emotional standoff, but the other half of me hopes she hasn't given up on me, because I wouldn't have given up on her.

I'm not sure if I'm elated or disappointed when I step into the bedroom, because a quick look around shows she's gone.

I climb into bed, and Chief jumps back up with me. He lies with his body pressed tight to the side of mine, and then he drifts off to doggie dreamland. I lie back on the pillows and catch the basketball scores, hoping I can get some sleep, because tomorrow, I have to meet with Ames's widow, and that is going to be a tough day full of emotional trauma, and I'm not sure that I can get through it without some sleep.

Who knows if it was the pills, the aromatherapy diffuser burning away in the corner, or the major orgasm that has me melting into the crappy hotel bed. Or maybe some combo of them all. But before I know it, I'm asleep with no dreams at all.

twenty-three

the wife and the mistress

Beep... *beep... beep...*
    I wipe the sleep away from my eyes and take a deep breath as I silence my alarm. I slept for the first time in a long time. Whether it was the pills or the aromatherapy, I don't care. I finally slept. And even though I don't feel rested, I feel a little better.

But it's when I pull back the covers and stand up that I remember what happened with Emma last night. How she had come to me, and I had been emotionally ripe for the picking, having just dreamed of the night she almost died on the living room floor. So when she knocked on the door and asked for me, I couldn't stop; I needed her too badly. I needed to reaffirm she was whole and vital, that her light was alive and bright and shining all around me.

It was amazing. And I will always want her. There will never be a time that I don't want her. And to be honest, I will never want another woman again after having Emma in my life and in my bed. But the tears in her eyes when I sent her away and she begged me to stay with her were enough to bring me to my knees.

I would have gone willingly if the bruise I gave her the other night wasn't still front and center on her beautiful face. Without its presence, I might have been able to convince myself it didn't happen, that I could trust myself around her and our children. But I needed the reminder that I can't. That if I'm in their lives, I will cause nothing but pain and heartbreak and misery. Emma and Hope and Ben deserve so much more than me.

I set the little hotel coffeemaker to brew while I take a quick shower. I showered last night, so this is just for the sake of shaking the last bit of fog of sleep from my brain. I towel off and pull on jeans and a T-shirt, my socks and boots, my favorite brown leather belt. I tuck my drop gun into my ankle holster and put my sidearm and badge on my belt.

I shoot back the cup of now lukewarm coffee that tastes and looks like mud, then grab my cell phone and my keys, and leave for the morning. My drive to the station is quiet. I don't turn on the radio; instead, I force myself to be present with my thoughts. I need to ground myself in the realization that I'm not good enough for my family. Then maybe I can find peace with what is left of my life. Or not.

As I pull into the station parking lot, my thoughts shift to Ames's widow. She's coming home today to take care of things, and Wes and I are meeting her at her home in an hour and a half. That's going to suck too. I've had Chief with me every day since Amy died. Will she want him back? Or will she let me buy him from her? As much as I miss and mourn my friend, I can't stand the thought of saying goodbye to Chief. He's always with me and a comforting balm to the loneliness that I no doubt deserve.

I park my car in my spot and badge my way into the office. Emma's car isn't here, but then again, this is one of the days that she works from home in order to be with the kids as much as possible. I wonder if that will change. Will she have to work more? I hope not. I'll see to it that she and the kids are taken care of. I don't want her to have to sacrifice just because I can't get my shit together.

I make my way into the kitchenette and grab a cup of coffee. It's not much better than the shit in the hotel, but I don't need gourmet. I just need enough caffeine to get the old synapses firing, and this tar will definitely do that.

I unlock my office and set my coffee down on my desk while I take off my jacket. I toss it on the rack by my door and then sit down behind my desk. I fire up my computer and drink my coffee while I check my email.

My office door flings open only slightly less than the last time he was here, and Wes steps in, letting the door shut behind him. He looks me over, and I get the distinct impression that he finds me lacking. *Well, get in fucking line, buddy. So do I.*

"I see you haven't fixed your shit yet," he drolls.

"What can I say?" I ask. "I'm a work in progress."

"Well, let's get to progressing a little faster," he says. "I'd hate to have to kick your ass for being a dumb fuck."

"Thank you," I murmur. "I really appreciate that grand show of your generosity."

"Good," he snaps. "You fucking should."

I let out a heavy sigh. "Are you ready to go see Stacy?"

He looks away and then turns back to me with a resolute expression on his face. "Yeah, and I'm driving. Your driving is as bad as your sister's."

"You take that back!"

"No," he says. "Now get your ass moving."

I grab my jacket off the coat hanger and slide it up my arms. The cool autumn breeze is just strong enough to sting a bit. I like it; it grounds me and keeps me present in the moment—something I'm struggling to do on my own right now.

He beeps the locks on his Uncle-Sam-issued fed-mobile, and I smirk. My sister gives him so much shit about being a Men in Black, suit-wearing fed that I don't need to. I didn't realize it at the time that it was because she hated him since he had broken her heart when she was barely more than a girl. Now it's like some weird kind of animal mating ritual between them. It's like watching their awkward foreplay. And that's gross.

"What's that look for?" he asks me.

"Oh, nothing," I reply as I pull open the passenger door of his sedan. "I was just thinking that everything Claire said about this car being a government piece of shit was absolutely true."

"Et tu, Lee?" he asks, clutching his heart like I've just betrayed him. He pulls out of the parking lot and drives us to meet our friend's widow.

"Hey, I'm not the one who went and became a fed," I start. When he growls a little, I ask, "Is this the day you hit me with your neuralizer so I don't remember that aliens walk among us?"

"Shut it."

"I can't," I add. "I need to know all the mysteries of the galaxy."

"Sometimes, I don't even know why we're friends," he says, rolling his eyes.

"And now," I reply with a ridiculous smile on my face, "we're family, because you knocked up my sister."

"That we are." He smirks as he pulls into Ames's driveway.

I push open my door, and Chief jumps out behind me and barks twice.

The three of us make our way up the long stone walkway that leads toward the front door. The one and the same that I blacked out on just two nights before. The dog sits down next to me and leans into my leg.

"Interesting," Wes mutters more to himself than to me before he raises his hand to knock on the door.

The three of us stand there and wait, but not for long, when Stacy pulls open the door. She looks older than the last time I saw her. Amy's death has clearly taken a heavy toll on her. Her blonde hair hangs limp around her shoulders, and her brown eyes are red-rimmed.

"Hey, Wes," she says as she pushes the door wide to allow us entry. "Lee. Come on in."

"Hey, Stacy," I greet her, and I follow her into the house.

"Have a seat," she says, and Wes and I both sit on the ends of the sofa. Chief sits next to me on the floor and leans into my legs. "Chief."

Stacy smiles sadly at the dog. She doesn't touch him, only sits in a chair across from us.

"How are you doing?" I ask, but we both know she feels like shit. Her world is falling apart, because her husband of sixteen years took his own life two nights ago.

"As well as can be expected," she answers. "The kids are really torn up."

"Where are they?" Wes asks.

"Back in South Carolina with my parents," she answers. There's nothing about her body language that says she's speaking anything but the truth. "I didn't want them to come back here and see this, and I'm glad they didn't. They lived enough of it while Jon was spiraling out of control."

"How long had Jon been suffering?" I ask.

"About a year ago, his nightmares were becoming an issue," she says. "About three months ago, a new counsellor came to the clinic at the VA, and he switched to seeing her from the older guy who runs the other group."

There's something about her tone of voice that has an electric current zinging down the back of my neck. Something isn't right here.

"Did you not like the guy who runs the other group?" Wes asks, having obviously picked up on the same thing I did.

"He was fine," she says, shrugging. "We had even seen him a couple of times together."

"Then why the strong feelings?" I ask, and her eyes bounce from Wes to me.

"You have to know…" she trails off.

"What should I know?" I ask, because something isn't right here. I don't know what it is yet, but something is not adding up.

"Jon was having an affair with his therapist," she says sadly.

"Are you sure?" Wes asks.

"I saw them here with my own two eyes," she replies. "I came home from the market one day, and he had her here, in our bed."

"I had no idea," I mumble. This doesn't sound like the same therapist who chastised me against using sex as a coping mechanism.

She shrugs again. "I figured you did. Jon said you were going to his group sessions now."

"I am."

She nods once and looks away. "Anyway, this has been a really trying time for me. I need to get his affairs in order, and then I need to get back to my kids so we can begin to move on with our lives."

"Absolutely," Wes says as he stands. "Thank you for your time."

"One last thing," I add as I stand. "I'd like to buy Chief from you."

She looks at me and then at the dog who is standing by my side. "He looks like he belongs with you," she says quietly. "Be good to each other. I'm sure you can see yourselves out."

"Yes, ma'am," Wes tells her, and then we walk to the door, and I do it with a huge weight taken off my shoulders because I get to keep Chief.

Too bad it's also with a belly full of acid churning, because something isn't adding up.

twenty-four

i won't give up

"**I** won't give up on us, Lee."

    "You should," I tell her. "I'm just not worth it anymore."

"Don't say that," she sobs.

"It's true, honey. I was broken a long time ago."

After we left Ames's house, Wes drove Chief and me back to the station to grab my vehicle. It was going to be another late takeout night, but tonight, it's going to go a little different. I need to get a run in to see if I can curb a lot of the tension that's pinging around in my body.

    "You going to be all right?" Wes asks me when he

pulls into a spot near mine.

"I don't know," I respond. "Stay tuned."

"That's not funny."

"It's not meant to be," I tell him. "I'm just being honest. I don't know yet, but I'm trying my damnedest."

"I know your sister would like to see you," he says. "Want to come over for dinner and see Claire and the kids?"

"I'll take a raincheck," I reply with a sigh. "Tonight, I need a run and a pizza."

"All right," he says quietly. "Just be happy."

"For now, I'd just settle for okay," I admit, and then I climb out of his car and hold the door open for Chief, who lopes after me as I make my way to my Tahoe.

I beep the locks with the button on my key fob and pull open the door. Chief and I hop in and head toward the shitty motel we now call our home. I pull into the lot and shut off the engine. Chief and I jog up the stairs, and I let us into the room.

I quickly strip out of my jeans and pull on a pair of running shorts and a hoodie. I lace up my running shoes and stuff some poop bags in my pocket. I stretch out my muscles and warm them up a bit, but it's no use; I still feel stiff. It's almost like I didn't sleep at all last night. There's so much tension in my neck and shoulders.

I give a quick whistle for Chief and hook up his

leash to his collar. I open the door to the room, and we make our way down the stairs and then start off on a brisk jog down the road. Jogging always used to clear my mind. I never minded PT, because it always helped me focus. But lately, I've been so disconnected that I'm not sure if anything can help me at this point. Not to mention that life has been so crazy since Hope was born and Emma was in the hospital recovering that I haven't found much time to work out. As my muscles burn as we make our way down the sidewalk, I can't help but realize what a mistake it was not to find time to clear my head and give my body a workout. I know it might seem awful, unthinkable, for me to leave her with two babies, but everyone will eventually see that it's better this way. It has to be this way. They aren't safe with me there. At least… not yet. But if I can get my shit together, then maybe, just maybe, I can get back to them and be the husband and father that they not only need me to be, but also deserve.

I try to think about where I went wrong. What mistakes I made and how I compounded them with my actions. And if there is a workaround. Can anything be done to save me, or am I just a lost cause? Emma doesn't think so, and neither does the rest of my family. But I hurt her. I caused her pain. How long until it's my sister or my nephew or my kids? My mom or my kind of mean grandma? They don't deserve the kind of hurt and destruction I now know I'm capable of.

My lungs are burning by the time Chief and I make it back to the motel. Although, he seems totally fine. We climb the metal steps to the second-story rooms, and I let us in with my room key.

Chief makes his way over to his bowls to slurp up some water while I order a pizza on my phone. I pour kibble in his bowl and then hit the shower. The lukewarm water does little to ease the tension in my muscles, but beggars can't be choosers. Although, a small voice in the back of my head whispers that I could be home right now taking a steaming-hot shower in the bathroom I designed. I could be with my family. I could be cuddling baby Hope or playing trains with Ben. I could hold Emma in my arms, make love to her, whisper my hopes and dreams for us and our children, if only I let myself.

And I do—I want it so bad that I can taste it. But somehow, someway, I ended up down this dark path, and I can't seem to find my way home, my way back to me. I don't need a perfect life. I know firsthand that nothing in life is perfect, but also, there's beauty to be found in the imperfect. I don't need a beacon on a lighthouse to guide my way home, but is a flashlight so much to ask for?

I finish my shower, turn off the taps, and grab a towel from the rack. I dry off my body and scrub the water from my hair before pulling on a pair of gray sweatpants and a T-shirt, just in time for the pizza to be delivered. I hand over cash to the delivery kid and tell him to keep the change before shutting the door behind me.

Usually, I love pizza. It's always been a favorite of mine. You can't grow up in New Jersey and not be able to appreciate a decent pie, and I love sharing one late in the evening after a long day at the station with Emma, but tonight, it sours in my gut.

I miss my girl. I miss my home. I miss my family.

And still, I know what I'm doing is right. I couldn't live with myself if something else happened to any one of them. No, this is for their own good. I'm protecting them.

I push aside the pizza and get up to brush my teeth. I look at the aromatherapy diffuser on the rickety motel desk and plug it in. I pour the oil mix Jane gave me into it and think again that maybe I don't know her as well as I thought I did. She should have known better than engaging in an extramarital affair with Ames, but then again, I shouldn't have slept with Anna and pursued Emma. I guess those who live in glass houses shouldn't throw stones.

I brush my teeth and take the stack of pills that she prescribed me. They take thirty minutes to set in, so I grab Chief's leash and take him out one last time. It's all fun and games until someone poops on the motel room floor.

He does his business quickly, and then we head back up the metal stairs for the last time tonight. I use my key to let us into the hotel room for the night and flip the latch and snap the chain in place. The room now swelters with the bitter smell of the essential oil blend, and the pills are starting to finally do their job. Here's hoping I can have one more night of decent rest, and then maybe I'll know what to do with my life in the morning.

My phone beeps with an incoming text. I pick it up and slide my finger across the screen to unlock it.

EMMA: Are you up?

I want to ignore her text. It hurts too much to have any kind of contact with Emma, but something could be wrong with one of the kids. Or her. Just because I don't want to hurt them doesn't mean I'm okay with anything else harming them too.

ME: Yeah. Are the kids all right?

EMMA: I think they miss you.

The little dots blink as she types out another message.

EMMA: I miss you too.

ME: I miss you guys too. It's better this way.

EMMA: It is not. Honey, please come home.

ME: You know I can't.

EMMA: I don't know anything.

ME: Is this why you messaged?

EMMA: No. I should have autopsy results on Jonathon Ames in the morning. I figured you'd like to know.

ME: Do you expect something other than suicide?

EMMA: No. But the state requires it. Hopefully, it can all be put to rest tomorrow.

ME: Yeah.

EMMA: I still miss you.

ME: I still miss you too.

EMMA: Come home, Lee.

ME: I can't.

EMMA: I love you.

ME: I love you too.

EMMA: Goodnight, honey.

ME: Goodnight.

I climb in the bed, and Chief hops up too. The pillows on the right side of the bed are his now. He curls up and tucks himself in, and then he begins to snore. I lay my arm across his belly lightly and count sheep jumping over the moon or whatever it is that will get me through the night.

As I lie there, I try and force each inch of my body to relax one by one. And then finally, I close my eyes and drift off to sleep.

"This was a major fuck-up."

Our commanding officer is pissed and rightfully so. This is a shitfuck of epic proportions. Our intel said the terrorist was hiding in the village, but when we got there, they were all dead.

"This op went so far FUBAR it's not remotely repairable," he keeps yelling.

We all stand silent, huddled around him.

"What do you want us to do now?" Ames asks.

"Nothing. Not one fucking thing."

"But—" Donovan starts.

"I said nothing," he growls in Rick's direction.

Ghost shoots him a look to tell him to shut up and back down before he finds his ass in a sling. Our CO is and has always been wound just a little too tight. He's not my favorite SEAL, but the team is where I belong, so I have to put up with his bullshit like everyone else.

"They were all dead when we got there," CO ex-plains—something we all know all too well in a way that the eyes of the dead will haunt me in my sleep. Not only was everyone dead, but so was my informant and her daughter.

I should have protected them, and I didn't.

I feel cold and wet against the back of my neck as I come awake. There is a heavy pressure along my back—a ninety-pound pressure.

Chief's whimper pulls me fully from the dream that has me in its grasp, and my breath saws in and out of my lungs.

"Fuck," I bite out.

The pills were supposed to help. The bullshit aro-matherapy was supposed to help, but it all feels like things are just getting worse and worse.

"Fuck."

Beep... beep... beeep...

My alarm sounds. I push out a heavy breath and get up to start my day. A day that is determined to suck right from the get-go. I have to admit that I'm not looking forward to Amy's autopsy findings. I still don't want to think of my friend as gone. He was always such a clown when we were overseas. If there was anyone who was capable of compartmentalizing the mission and its dangers to unwind a little, it was Amy. The fact that he couldn't battle the demons within never made sense to me. I guess I'll just never know what went on in his head that night. Then again, I hope I never do. If there's one thing I want more than anything else in this world, it's to find the strength to pull my shit together so I can return home to my family. I don't ever want to sink so low that I can't come back. That's my biggest fear, that maybe, just maybe, I'm already too far gone.

I get up and take a quick shower before dressing in jeans and a button-down shirt. I weave my belt through the loops on my jeans and then pull on my socks and boots. I clip my badge and my sidearm to my belt and tuck my drop gun into my ankle holster. I pocket my phone and my wallet and grab my keys.

I whistle for Chief and clip his leash to his collar and then lead him down the stairs to the Tahoe where it sits in the parking lot. I beep the locks on my key fob and hold open the door for Chief to hop in.

The drive to the station is a quiet one. I pull into my spot at the back of the station, and I shut off the engine. Chief and I climb down from the truck, and I use my badge to unlock the door and let us in. We walk down the hallway to the kitchenette, where I pour a cup of stale coffee and then head to my office.

Chief settles in on the floor of my office with his favorite chew toy. I sit down in my chair at my desk and watch him for a minute while my old as hell computer boots up. I can't believe how relaxed he keeps me, how in tune to my moods and emotional state he is. He's highly unusual for a service dog. Most would not switch from one person to another so seamlessly, but here he is, pulling me out of anxiety attacks and nightmares. I know it's only been a few days, but I'd be lost without him.

I spend the next few hours checking in with my officers and detectives and catching up on reports. Everything looks good. There doesn't seem to be a ton going on, and it doesn't really feel like any of them need me right now. Usually, there's always some kind of tiff here or there. Someone has stepped on someone else's toes, or no one has turned in their reports. Honestly, most of the time, it feels like herding a bunch of feral cats with high testosterone levels, a job that would make anyone crazy. But lately, they all have their shit together, and I can't help but feel like I'm the only one who doesn't.

The phone on my desk rings, and I pick up. "Goodnite."

"It's me," Emma says when I answer. "I have the final reports from the lab."

"I'm on my way," I say before I hang up. I don't want to go down to her lab, but I have no choice. This is how we've always done things here. And I can't stop doing my job just because I'm heartbroken for the sexy medical examiner. So, I have to suck it up. I have to go down there and be a professional.

Chief stands when I do, always alert to my every move. We make our way out of my office and down the hall to the stairs. I feel too on edge to take the elevator today. I push open the stairwell door, and Chief and I jog down the stairs. From here, there is a fire door that opens outside her office, where if we had taken the elevator, it would open inside her office. Whoever designed this station was a bit of a nut. Not much makes sense, but then again, no one has ever questioned it either.

"There you are," she says with a gentle smile on her gorgeous face for me.

"Hey."

"Come on in," she says before dropping down to scratch behind Chief's ears. "Hey, buddy."

"The autopsy?" I ask, and Chief groans as he lies down on the floor. It's times like these I wonder if he actually flunked out of service doggie school and Amy got him at half price. He definitely has character; that's for sure.

"Well, for starters, primary cause of death is death by hanging," she says, looking at me. I steel my spine against the soft pitying look that crosses over her face. Ames is dead and gone. I know that. I also know there is no bringing him back either. "You okay?"

"I'm fine."

"Okay," she says softly. "He had well over normal levels of alcohol, anxiety medications, and various homeopathic remedies in his body."

"That's not more than we had found front and center on his coffee table and littered all over the floor," I remind her.

"That is true," she says, but ever the scientist, my girl isn't happy until she's solved every puzzle and has an answer for everything. Jesus, she's so fucking smart it blows me away. "But the levels of camphor, hemlock, and yellow jasmine were all found in his lungs, his brain, and I also swabbed his nasal cavities, and there was a heavy presence there too."

"What could those do?" I ask.

"Well, the levels that he inhaled and ingested are enough to cause extreme anxiety and even psychosis," she explains. "Can you think of any reason why he would be inhaling deadly substances?

"He was being treated for psychosis," I explain. "The clinic at the VA encourages therapy, medication, and aromatherapy. Sounds like that could explain it."

"Yes and no," she says. "While camphor is more common than the others, yellow jasmine and water hemlock are extremely toxic. They can be very deadly."

"This sounds like poor Amy was set up in a perfect storm just waiting for tragedy," I reply, and Emma watches me closely.

"Yeah," she agrees, and a funny look crosses her face. "I guess I just have a funny feeling about it."

"I wouldn't spend too much thought on it," I reply. "None of it will bring Amy back."

"I know that, Lee," she says, reaching out and laying a hand on my arm. "It's you I want back."

"Emma—" I start, but she interrupts me with her soft voice.

"Come back to me, Lee."

She leans into me, wrapping her arms around my shoulders, and presses her mouth to mine. I know I should resist her, that I should turn around and walk away, but there is something about Emma Parker that draws me in. I can't be near her and not have her, not hear her voice and listen to her thoughts. I love this woman, and there is nothing I can do to stay away. It's why I had to leave in the first place. I would never be able to stay strong down the hall or on the sofa. I have to be near her, to touch her and taste her.

I lick into her mouth and deepen the kiss. Emma whimpers down my throat as she runs her palm down the front of my jeans, and my cock fills and hardens under her touch.

I back her toward the desk and lean her over it. She wraps her legs around my hips and grinds her covered pussy over my hard length. I growl and trail my lips down the side of her neck and nip her behind her ear as she slides the zipper down on my jeans and pulls me free from my pants. She wraps her tight fist around my hard cock and strokes me twice. I pull away from her before this is over before it even begins.

She slides her hands up the back of my T-shirt and rakes her nails down my back. The sting makes me focus on nothing but her. I'm consumed by her. I pull the drawstring of her scrub pants loose and pull them down her legs. She kicks out of her sneakers and lets them drop to the floor.

She lets her legs fall open, exposing herself to me. Her pink petals glisten, and I want her more than I want air to breathe.

"Please, honey," she breathes as she pulls me into her. I notch the tip of my cock to her opening and press inside her. "Yes."

She tosses her head back and leans on her elbows when I slide out and drive back in. Slowly, oh so slowly, I pull out and then drive back in. We hold onto each other as I pound in and out of her. Papers slide all around her desk.

Emma wraps her legs around my waist and digs her heels into my ass as I plunge into her body over and over again. My mouth hovers over hers, and we breathe each other in. I need her. I have never needed anyone like this, not ever.

"Yes," she pants, and I feel the first flutters as her pussy contracts around my cock.

I move faster and faster, driving harder, and I'm determined to push her over the edge. The legs of the desk scrape and groan across the floor of her office.

Her nails bite into the skin of my back, and her neck and face flush the most beautiful pink as she comes. I drive deep again and again, and then I plant myself inside her to the root and follow her over the edge.

I keep her wrapped up in my arms, me wrapped up in her, my favorite place to be as we both struggle to catch our breath. I let my head tip forward so my forehead rests against hers. Skin to skin while I'm still buried deep inside her, connected in the most primal of ways.

"I'll never let you go, Lee," she whispers, and I press my eyes closed tight. "I won't give up."

"I'm not sure I'm worth the fight," I whisper harshly, and it's true. One of my biggest worries is that I'm unworthy of the effort at all.

"You are worth so much more, honey," she says. "And I'm not going to give up. Not now, not ever."

I nod once, unsure what to do with her faith in me. Is it blind trust? I just don't know.

"I need to get back to work," I say sadly.

"I know," she agrees.

I slip from her body and do up my pants. I pick up her scrub pants, roll them up in my hands, and slide each leg up her gently. Reverently, I tie the drawstring on her pants for her after she shimmies them up her hips. I slip her sneakers on each foot, just like she's my real-life Cinderella, and then I place a soft kiss on her lips.

"I'm sorry," I whisper as tears pool in her green eyes. "I love you; I do. I just don't know what to do."

"I know," she says sadly, and the first tear slips free. "I love you too. I always will."

I can see it's tearing her up that she can't help me. Emma can't solve these problems for me and make it all go away. I know she would if she could, but the fact that my struggles are so far removed from things that she can control, she can't help it.

And she hates it.

And I hate that this is just another way I have hurt her.

So I turn on my heels with Chief jumping up to follow me. I jog up the stairs and to my office to collect my belongings and clip Chief's lead to his collar, and then we head out into the late afternoon. Maybe some fresh air will help the feeling that the walls are closing in on me. Maybe it won't. All I know is that I have to get out of this station and away from the woman I love before I do something else I will regret.

Famous last words, right?

twenty-five

over and over

My thoughts spin out of control the whole way back to the motel. It feels like there is a tight band wrapped around my chest, and my heart seems like it's beating too fast in my chest. Sweat beads up on my lip, my hairline, and the back of my neck, and I'm hoping against all hope that I make it to my motel room before I hurl up the coffee that's currently eating its way through my stomach lining.

Chief keens in the back seat as I make my way through town. *Fuck, please don't let me pass out again.* I just have to make it through one more stoplight, and then I'm home free. It's red as I approach the intersection, and I begin to panic, but then the light turns green.

I pull into the lot and park my car as close to the stairs as I can. I cut the engine and grab my keys from the ignition. I climb down from the Tahoe, and Chief jumps out after me. Black spots begin to burst at the edge of my vision as I climb the stairs.

I can't catch my breath, and it feels like I'm having a heart attack.

I use my key to let us into the motel room, and Chief is still whining. My head is beginning to pound, and the sound of his crying is like an ice pick on my brain.

I drop my badge and gun on the nightstand and strip off my clothes. I'll do anything to make this feeling go away. I flip the switch on the aromatherapy diffuser and let it start cranking while I fill a paper coffee cup in the bathroom sink and shake out a bunch of pills from the various bottles on the bathroom counter. I toss a bunch of them in my mouth and wash them down with the weird-tasting water.

I drop the cup on the counter and pace around the room. What the fuck is wrong with me? Why do I feel this way? Fuck, I'm such a mess. Thank Christ I left the station before Emma could see me this way again. I hate that she saw me pass out at Ames's house. When did I become so weak? It's fucking embarrassing. I used to be a warrior. Now? Now, I'm nothing.

The pills are finally starting to work, and a slow rolling warmth coasts over my body and through it. Finally, I feel sleepy. So I pull back the rough blankets, lie down, and finally, fucking finally, close my eyes and drift off to sleep.

"This was a major fuck-up."

Our commanding officer is pissed and rightfully so. This is a shitfuck of epic proportions. Our intel said the terrorist was hiding in the village, but when we got there, they were all dead.

"This op went so far FUBAR it's not remotely repairable," he keeps yelling.

We all stand silent, huddled around him.

"What do you want us to do now?" Ames asks.

"Nothing. Not one fucking thing."

"But—" Donovan starts.

"I said nothing," he growls in Rick's direction.

Ghost shoots him a look to tell him to shut up and back down before he finds his ass in a sling. Our CO is and has always been wound just a little too tight. He's not my favorite SEAL, but the team is where I belong, so I have to put up with his bullshit like everyone else.

"They were all dead when we got there," CO explains—something we all know all too well in a way that the eyes of the dead will haunt me in my sleep. Not only was everyone dead, but so was my informant and her daughter.

I should have protected them, and I didn't.

I didn't protect them.

I didn't protect them. I didn't protect them.

I said that I would protect them. We promised. We promised to protect them, and we didn't. The memories swirl through my brain over and over.

We said we would protect them, and we didn't. And then we swore we wouldn't say a word. I should have done something then when I knew in my gut that something was off. I always trust my gut, but for whatever reason then, I didn't.

Now it's too late.

They're dead. They're all dead.

And on that happy thought, sleep takes me under again.

Eyes.

The smell of sulfur fills my nostrils, and smoke sears my lungs. The heavy weight of the rifle in my hands is like second nature to me. I could carry it in my sleep. During training, I probably did.

But it's the eyes that chill me to the bone in the middle of this hot desert.

I don't know how the intel had gone so bad. I know

it happens, but not like this. One minute, the mission was going to plan, and the next, the world exploded. Spurts of gunfire can be heard all around me, but it's the screams that ring in my ears.

"Fuck, fuck, fuck!" I hear Adams scream through the comm in my ear. "They're dead. They're all dead."

And he's right. They're all dead. Every last one of them. I was helpless to prevent this, and still I feel like I should have. It's as bad as if their blood was directly on my hands.

I make my way through the village we've been watching, my heart in my throat. Buildings, homes, the carts in the market, they're all gone, burned-out shells of what they were before. And bodies crumpled where they fell. Men, women, children, death does not discriminate. Their eyes vacant after life left them.

If eyes are the window to the soul, then this is a portal to hell as I look at the faces of each person who should not have died. A child we gave a candy bar to yesterday, an old woman who offered coffee in the market, and a beautiful young woman whose belly was swollen with a baby.

Her dark eyes watch me, haunt me, as she sees me and nothing at all. And then they change to the green of Emma's, her belly cut open and our child just gone. I was helpless to stop it. I should have known what would happen. I should have protected them, but I didn't.

The smoke burns my throat as I turn to the left and see Emma's blonde-and-pink hair, her green eyes open and watching me, her beautiful body mutilated, because I was in her life.

"No!" I shout.

But the eyes of the dead scream that this is all my fault.

It's all my fault.

It's all my fault… all my fault. I hurt everyone I've ever known. When will I learn? Everything is all my fault.

Without me, Anna would still be alive.

Without me, my informant and her young daughter would still be alive.

Everyone is dead because of me.

It's all my fault.

All my fault.

All my fucking fault.

And then sleep claims me again, and I relive my penance of watching every life I've ruined, every mistake I've ever made, play on a loop in my brain over and over again.

It's all my fault.

It's all my fault.

The smell of sulfur fills my nostrils, and smoke sears my lungs. The heavy weight of the rifle in my hands is like second nature to me. I could carry it in my sleep. During training, I probably did.

But it's the eyes that chill me to the bone in the middle of this hot desert.

I don't know how the intel had gone so bad. I know it happens, but not like this. One minute, the mission was going to plan, and the next, the world exploded. Spurts of gunfire can be heard all around me, but it's the screams that ring in my ears.

"Fuck, fuck, fuck!" I hear Adams scream through the comm in my ear. "They're dead. They're all dead."

And he's right. They're all dead. Every last one of them. I was helpless to prevent this, but still I feel like I should have. It's as bad as if their blood was directly on my hands.

The smoke burns my throat as I turn to the left and see Emma's blonde-and-pink hair, her blue eyes open and watching me, her beautiful body mutilated, because I was in her life.

"No!" I shout.

But the eyes of the dead scream that this is all my fault.

"It's all my fault," I mumble. My throat is raw from the smoke inhalation and the screams echo in my ears, but still, I know that's not right, right?

"That's right," a familiar voice coos. "It's all your fault."

"My fault."

"Yes, Captain Goodnite. It's your fault, and now you have to pay."

"It was you," I gasp as I fade in and out of consciousness as the noose tightens around my neck when it's pulled tight. "It was all you."

"Yes." They laugh. "It was all me."

"Not my fault."

"Oh no, it's very much your fault, and now you're going to die."

And then she raises my hand holding my gun to my head. Where did that come from? I locked it away, didn't I? I can't remember... I can't remember.... The memories, that's all I remember.

"It's you," I say, blinking my eyes to try to clear them. "It was you all along."

"Of course," she says with a smile on her face.

"Ames?" I ask.

"That was me," she admits, her smile widening, and my brain spins and spins. It can't be just me and Amy. There have to be more.

"Palmer?"

"That was me too." She shrugs. "Eventually, you're all going to die. And I'm going to make that happen.

It's the least I can do. We both know you deserve it."

I wasn't ready to go, but I guess it's like they say, *"Life's a bitch, and then you die."*

twenty-six

true believer

Thirty minutes earlier

It's time.

    I have waited and waited and waited, and now, Captain Goodnite is mine. I could hardly believe my luck that he seemed to be spiraling out of control so quickly.

    Then again, I did up the toxic elements in his oil diffuser. The quantities I had given him were much higher than those I had given to Jonathon Ames. Mr. Ames took quite a long time to lose his mind. I had planned to let Captain Goodnite suffer slowly as well, but then again, it would appear that I don't have much patience after all.

    I also tampered with his medications. The herbal supplements for anxiety were nothing but water hem-

lock and yellow jasmine dried down and ground up and mixed with a little LSD for fun. The combination was a recipe for hallucinations, nightmares, and psychosis. Nothing like a little California Sunshine to help move things along.

I figure if it was good enough to get a bunch of hippies in the '60s to jump off buildings, it was good enough to help me put down a bunch of uniform-wearing thugs. Because that's what they are. Thugs. They put on their uniforms and parade around as heroes, when they are anything but. Monsters. Wolves in sheep's clothing. Anything is better than a hero. They are supposed to protect people. To do right and protect good from evil, but is that really what they are? Is there really evil out there, or is it only those on the losing side of history labeled things like evil or terrorist? These men are the true monsters.

And I loved watching every minute of their demise.

But now, it's time to get the show on the road. I have an entire SEAL team to kill. Infiltrating each of their lives takes countless hours of planning to make sure I cannot only get to them, but also do it without suspicion.

I was fortunate that Jonathon led Captain Goodnite right to my door, but next time I won't be so lucky. I'm going to have to disappear for a while before I can make a play on Agent O'Connell. Maybe a car accident? That sounds divine. After all, he does put away a lot of very bad people. I bet it's not outside of the realm of possibility that, say, one of those very bad people were to be angry. Maybe even so angry they would be moved to cut the brake lines on his car.

After that, I'll devote some time to finding the man who they call the surfer. I don't remember much about him, only whispers here and there. After they all left the teams, he went on to work for an organization that scrubbed his very existence. He's going to take me some time to get a lock on. But never fear. I'm determined to succeed.

But that is not for now.

Now, Captain Goodnite is about to die.

I waited for him outside the station at a safe distance. And I watched as he and that damn dog ran out of the building like their tails were on fire. I followed him all the way back to the seedy motel he's been staying in ever since he walked out on his family, leaving him isolated and right where I want him. His driving was erratic at best. Captain Goodnite is clearly unravelling.

I parked across the lot and watched and waited. I'm good at those things. I've been watching and waiting my entire fucking life.

He stumbled at the landing as he raced up the rickety metal steps that lead up to the second floor, where his room is located. I've known where he was the entire time.

Lights flashed on behind the curtains. The door haphazardly slammed. He's not going anywhere, and now, he's mine.

I step out of my car and smile at the beggar on the corner. No one will believe her if she manages to be coherent enough to tell the authorities anything about my visit tonight.

I take my time as I walk through the parking lot. I'm not in a hurry. There's no rush. Only time to savor this moment. Captain Goodnite has been a worthy opponent. His moral compass and inner strength led him away from my true direction over and over, but now it all comes down to who the ultimate victor is, and I am the true believer. My mission is held above all else, because there is nothing more important in this life than righting a wrong, than seeking vengeance.

My heels click on the metal stairs as I ascend the path toward the captain's final destination. He never should have entered that village all those years ago. And he definitely should have kept the promise he made way back when. Instead, he chose wrong, and now he has to pay.

I walk down the hall and see a maid is cleaning a room a few doors down. She's not paying any attention to her housekeeping cart that is parked right outside the door. Music blares from inside the room, and I can hear her off-key singing. Through the crack in the door, I catch glimpses of movement as she dances along to her songs while she works.

I spy, hanging from the corner of the cart, just what I need. She's so immersed in her duties that she shouldn't mind my liberating the item for just a little bit. I snatch her master room key from where it hangs and quietly make my way back to the captain's room.

I slide it in the card reader, and the light turns green as the lock unlatches. I gently push the door open and see Captain Goodnite and his dog sprawled on the bed. The captain is unconscious, but the dog picks his head up and emits a low growl.

"It's all right, boy," I say quietly. Holding up my hands in front of me, I approach the dog, but he continues to growl. This could be a problem.

Never fear. If anything, I am determined. My nose burns as the diffuser burns the toxic oils, and I spy the pill bottles open on the bathroom counter. By the looks of things, the captain has gotten his sendoff party started smashingly. I can't wait.

I didn't choose this life, this path, but fate chose it for me.

I am the judge, the jury, and the executioner.

And Captain Liam Goodnite is about to die.

twenty-seven

not right

EMMA

Something is not right here. I don't know what it is, but it's not adding up. Maybe it's because I don't yet have all of the pieces of the puzzle in front of me yet. Maybe it's because I miss Lee and I want him back.

It feels like we finally got our life together. After circling each other for years, Lee and I were like two magnets being pulled together by forces beyond our control. When Anna was part of our sad love triangle, I had no hope. I was desperately in love with a man who was in love with me, but one of my closest friends was also in love with him. I would never go there while she was in the picture, and although Lee didn't feel the same way, she felt the pull of him like I did.

Once you're caught in Liam Goodnite's sexual tractor beams, there is no hope for your pussy or your heart. She was as good as gone, and sadly, so was I.

After she died, I was so wracked with guilt. I felt responsible for her death, for the way her life ended. And as awful as it sounds, I blamed Lee too. If only he could have loved her and not me. Anna would still be alive today. I felt it was our feelings for each other that murkied the water, and it took me a long time to understand that just wasn't the case.

I needed to wrap my mind around the fact that without things happening the way they did, the grief and the loss, the guilt, and the passion wouldn't have built up so high they boiled over by the water after Wes and Claire's wedding. And if Lee and I hadn't given in to those feelings, if we hadn't been so overcome with emotions when the alcohol took away our inhibitions, we wouldn't have made Hope. And after all, what is life without Hope?

But our story didn't come together then. Oh no. I fought the pull. I wanted to stay feeling like shit. I didn't want to believe we could have it all. That we deserved to have it all or the right to try to work at it and fight for it. I lied to Lee and to me about everything under the sun, including Hope's paternity, and still, he fought for me.

I had to give in, and it was the sweetest loss ever. A victory we both relished, because in the end, we got to be together. I finally had a family, something I had never experienced before. Growing up in foster homes doesn't nurture loving family bonds like on TV. But with Lee, I had it all.

And then when Hope was born and I was attacked, it was like someone flipped a switch inside Lee. He started having more nightmares. I always had a feeling he had a level of PTSD he just managed with sheer will and determination. The occasional nightmares are nothing out of the norm for a veteran like him. But this became more.

I thought when he began seeing the shrink at the VA that things would take a turn for the better… only they didn't. He was coping, but he was also spiraling out of control, and I was helpless to stop it. I would do anything in my power to stop it if I could.

Having another baby in the house seemed to push the already over-exhausted Lee over the edge. I hate that Ben could be part of the catalyst to Lee's downfall. But I still don't regret it. I love Lee, and I love Ben and Hope, and I would do it all again just to have them in my life. I love them that much.

The night Ames died, I thought we were on an upswing, that things were going to get better, but they didn't. Lee's panic attack at Ames's home, seeing his body the way it was should have been a sign that the situation had deteriorated past my control, but still, I tried.

When he lost control later that night and hit me, I could see it in his eyes that he was gone. His light was extinguished, and the pain he felt over harming me— whether on purpose or accidental—was palpable. And

212 | jennifer rebecca

the sad part is, it was my fucking fault. I knew better. I shouldn't have touched him like that. I knew not to try to pull him from a nightmare, but I was convinced I could save him.

And how wrong I was.

I learned the hard way that my man is stubborn, and once he's decided something, he sticks to it. So when he decided to leave me under the guise that it was for my own good, I knew he was going to see it through. And like a fucking idiot, I let him go.

If ever there was anyone meant for me and me for them, it's Lee.

But that's neither here nor there. I guess I hoped to be able to give him some closure with these autopsy results, and still, I left him with nothing. The panic in his eyes as he ripped himself away from me was devastating. I think it might be time for me to realize I'm doing him more damage than good. And besides, it's obliterating my heart to keep trying.

But now that I'm in deep in these lab results, I have more questions than answers, and that is something I do not like.

The elevator dings as its doors open, and Wes steps out. He smiles at me. Wes has been looking after the kids and me, checking in on us since Lee moved out. And he hasn't exactly hid his displeasure at his best friend's actions either. While I wish he would go easier on Lee, I also can't blame him. If he had treated Claire the way Lee treated me, I'd have him by his balls. No doubt about it.

"Hey, Em," he greets me. "Have you seen Lee?"

"Hey, Wes," I reply. "You missed him earlier."

"Shit."

"What's up?" I ask.

"I keep going over Ames's file, and I end up with more questions than I have answers," he replies.

"You and me both, buddy," I say as I wave my hand over the toxicology and autopsy reports on my desk. "You go first. Maybe we can add all of our puzzle pieces together and see what comes out of it."

"That's not a bad idea," he says. "I was hoping he could answer some questions about the therapist who leads the group sessions at the VA clinic. I went to look into her, and there is literally nothing from about six months ago back."

"Really?" I ask. "That's weird."

"It is. Not to mention, she was having an affair with Ames."

"You're joking," I gasp.

"I wish I was," he says sadly. "Stacy was always one of the best of the team's wives."

"That blows," I mumble.

"It really does," he says. "So what has you stumped over a suicide?"

"It's weird," I start.

"What's weird?" he asks, and I wave him to where

I'm standing over my desk, looking at the information as it's laid out all over the top of the battered wood.

"This," I say, motioning to the toxicology reports. "Jonathon Ames was a dead man walking, but I'm not sure the primary cause was mental illness from PTSD."

"What do you mean?" Wes asks me. "Explain this to me."

"His blood alcohol volume was off the charts, yes, and that is not a great start," I explain. "His body was full of anti-anxiety meds along with antidepressants."

"There was plenty of evidence of both at his house, so that can't be what has you questioning things," he comments.

"His body was also full of camphor, water hemlock, and yellow jasmine among other things," I add.

"What are those?"

"In short, toxic plants."

"And what would they do?"

"Each of those can cause anxiety, hallucinations, night terrors, and psychosis," I explain. "Together, they're a recipe for hell on earth."

"And why would he have those in his body?"

"That's what I don't get. He shouldn't have had them in his body at all, and definitely not in the amounts he had."

"Where could they have come from?" Wes asks.

"Lee said the therapist gave him an aromatherapy

diffuser with a custom blend of oils and herbs to help promote relaxation," I explain.

"Do you think that's what did it?"

"I don't know," I answer. "But I'd like to find out."

"Then let's hit it," he says. "We can go visit Lee really quick and then get some much-needed answers."

"There's one other thing," I begin.

"What's that?"

"Jonathon Ames also had high levels of lysergic acid diethylamide in his body."

"LSD?" he asks. "That's odd."

"It is," I reply. "Because it's common knowledge that LSD causes hallucinations, but also mental dissociation and psychopathy."

"Sounds like a real fun time," he says. "But why would someone suffering from PTSD or other issues take something like that?"

"That's the thing," I say. "I don't think they knowingly would."

"Shit," he bites out. "We missed it."

"We all did. But also, it can cause an increased homicidal or suicidal risk."

"So you think Ames had help?" he asks me. "Honest opinion."

"Honest opinion," I answer, "I think I pulled the file on Palmer from your office and his toxicology report looks exactly the same. I think they both had help."

"You're shitting me."

"I wish I were."

"I was on the initial investigation into Palmer's death, because I knew him," he says. "But he didn't die in New Jersey. Palmer was living in Virginia at the time."

"I know."

"And he was attending group therapy sessions regularly at the local VA hospital, but when we went to question his therapist, she had left with no forwarding address," he says. "I think we need to find Lee. Now."

"Do you think he's in danger?" I ask, but I'm already on the move, grabbing my coat and my bag.

"Yeah, honey, I do," he says gently.

I follow Wes up the stairs, through the station, and out the back door. We climb in his car, and he peels out of the parking lot.

I hold onto the dash and the door handle as he races across town to the motel where Lee has been staying the last few nights. Please, God, let us get to him in time. I can't live without him.

I turn to Wes and say, "I think it's time you told me what happened overseas."

twenty-eight

it's okay to not be okay

LEE

I t's all my fault.

The smell of sulfur fills my nostrils, and smoke sears my lungs. The heavy weight of the rifle in my hands is like second nature to me. I could carry it in my sleep. During training, I probably did.

But it's the eyes that chill me to the bone in the middle of this hot desert.

I don't know how the intel had gone so bad. I know it happens, but not like this. One minute, the mission was going to plan, and the next, the world exploded. Spurts of gunfire can be heard all around me, but it's the screams that ring in my ears.

"Fuck, fuck, fuck!" I hear Adams scream through

the comm in my ear. "They're dead. They're all dead."

And he's right. They're all dead. Every last one of them. I was helpless to prevent this, but still, I feel like I should have. It's as bad as if their blood was directly on my hands.

The smoke burns my throat as I turn to the left and see Emma's blonde-and-pink hair, her green eyes open and watching me, her beautiful body mutilated, because I was in her life.

"No!" I shout.

But the eyes of the dead scream that this is all my fault.

"It's all my fault," I mumble. My throat is raw from the smoke inhalation, and the screams echo in my ears, but still, I know that that's not right, right?

"That's right," a familiar voice coos. "It's all your fault."

"My fault."

"Yes, Captain Goodnite. It's your fault, and now you have to pay."

"It was you," I gasp. "It was all you."

"Yes." They laugh. "It was all me."

"Not my fault."

"Oh no, it's very much your fault, and now you're going to die."

And then she raises my hand holding my gun to

my head. Where did that come from? I locked it away, didn't I? I can't remember… I can't remember…. The memories, that's all I remember.

"It's you," I say, blinking my eyes to try to clear them. "It was you all along."

"Of course," she says with a smile on her face.

"Ames?" I ask.

"That was me," she admits, her smile widening, and my brain spins and spins. It can't be just me and Amy. There have to be more.

"Palmer?"

"That was me too." She shrugs. "Eventually, you're all going to die. And I'm going to make that happen. It's the least I can do. We both know you deserve it."

"I don't understand," I mumble. Why me? Why kill my friends? I don't understand.

"I can see you don't remember me," she says.

"Who are you?"

She seems to think about my question for a second before answering.

"I guess I can tell you that," she says. "While my name isn't important to the story, you need to know where I come from. I was born in a small, remote village in the Afghan Province."

I close my eyes against the knowing stare of those who I had been seeing in my dreams every night for the last several months. Only I didn't realize it at the time, because in my dream, her dark eyes morph from hers, to Anna's, to Emma's before I wake. I had thought that they were the eyes of the dead, but I was wrong. While her mother died that day protecting her, it would appear *she* had not. And we had left her for dead.

"I see that you're remembering," she says with a broad smile. "I thought you would save me. I was awake and listening when you told my mother you would protect us. You didn't."

"I didn't know—" I start, but she cuts me off.

"Didn't know what?" she bites out. "That I was alive?"

"No."

"That my father was the terrorist you were looking for?"

"What?" I ask, because there was no knowledge of that in the intel we had. No chatter suggested that her mother was informing the U.S. government on her own husband.

"Yes," she says. "Your commanding officer was paid handsomely by my father to leave out certain pieces of information. My father, the bastard he was, was very enterprising like that."

"But why? I-I don't understand."

"You convinced her that you were doing right," she says. "That you would protect her. And. She. Died."

She wraps her hand around mine, and I feel the cool metal of my drop gun in our combined grasp. Shit. Fuck. I must not have locked it up. I wasn't feeling right. I wasn't thinking straight.

"With a little mixed medications and some questionable pharmacology and aromatherapy, it was like shooting fish in a barrel. Like I'm going to shoot you," she says, and I feel our hands tighten around the trigger. "Or I guess I should say, like you're going to shoot yourself."

I close my eyes and offer up a prayer that Emma knows how much I love her, how much I have always loved her. That she'll be able to move on from this, from me, and she'll be able to guide our children toward a beautiful life. And that most of all, she's happy. That's all I have ever wanted for her, for the kids.

I feel her apply more pressure to my hand. This gun isn't an easy one. And I think she's just about got it when the door to the room splinters apart.

"No!" Emma screams as she tackles Jane. Wes is right behind her, grabbing and pulling me off the bed from the other side and out of the way as the gun goes off.

A searing pain rips through the side of my neck and my upper arm.

I watch helplessly, unable to move from whatever drugs I ingested, as Emma grabs the large aromatherapy diffuser and smashes it over Jane's head just moments before she collapses.

I drift in and out.

"It's okay, honey," Emma says. "Help is on the way."

"Okay," I mumble just before everything goes black again.

Twenty-four hours later

Beep... beep... beep... beep...

My eyelids feel like sandbags are weighting them down. I fight against the heavy pull of unconsciousness as the steady beeps pound along with the thump of my heart, and my lungs push and pull oxygen in and out of my body.

The lights in the room are blazing bright white. I blink. And then I blink again. I look down my body and see it's wrapped tight in a hospital gown and blankets. I'm in a hospital bed.

Shit.

I turn my head to the side and see Emma sitting in a chair next to my bed. Her hands are small and warm and hold tight to mine as she leans over where they're joined on the bed beside me. She looks small and fragile, and I hate that I scared her.

I squeeze her hand, and her head pops up. She blinks away the last fingers of sleep and smiles at me.

"Hey," she whispers.

"Hey."

"Should I call someone?" she asks.

"Not yet," I answer. I just want a moment to look at her, to drink her in. Without the toxins and drugs in my body, I still feel anxiety, but it's not unbearable. I realize how close I was to losing everything that's important to me.

"Okay," she says softly.

"I'm sorry," I whisper, and it comes out harsh and pained. She looks at me for a beat, her face softening, and then she proceeds to rock my world.

"You have nothing to be sorry for," Emma replies.

"But—"

"It's okay to not be okay," she says. "It's okay to have bad days, to live in hard seasons. When you've been through the things you and I have, it's expected to have those things happen. But we have to get up and keep fighting, keep living our lives every day, whether it's hard or it's easy. We have to keep living."

"You're right."

"I know." She winks at me. "And you have to know I will never give up on you."

"I hope you never do," I say, and the emotion has welled up in my throat that it's audible in my voice.

"I love you, Lee," she says. "I always will."

"I'll always love you."

"Good," she replies as she settles into the hospital bed next to me. "Now, don't you think it's time you let me make an honest man out of you once and for all?"

"Yeah. I think it's about time."

"Good," she says with a soft smile for me on her face that shines through her eyes. "Because I have an idea."

twenty-nine

the gift

Two weeks later

The sun is just beginning to disappear from the sky, leaving a painted trail of pinks and oranges in its wake. It's the perfect backdrop for a wedding—my wedding.

I'm standing under a heavy willow tree in my parents' backyard with Wes standing beside me. A local judge we know is presiding today. He's an older fellow, small in stature but a lion in the courtroom, and as nice as can be. Ben sits on my hip in his baby suit. His head is tipped back as he watches the hundreds of crystals and rose blooms that hang from ribbons in the boughs of the tree overhead, where they sparkle and spin in the breeze.

It's hard to think that just two weeks ago, I almost

lost my life to a serial killer. Once Wes knew who to look for, he discovered she had scores of photos tapes to the walls and pictures crossed out with lipstick. She had been following members of our SEAL team including Jake and Rick. She was even planning to get to them once Jake left the White House. It was enough to give anyone nightmares.

Wes thinks she's going to get the death penalty but it's a tricky situation. As her father was a known terrorist and her mother, my informant all those years ago, she is not a U.S. national and there for not subject to our courts. Either way, I'll never be seeing her again.

I wish I had known that she was alive and under her mother. Maybe I could have saved us all, who knows? All I know is that Palmer and Amy didn't deserve to die like that. No one does. No one should feel helpless and alone like that and I will do everything I can to see that men and women like us get the help that they need.

Until then, I hope she suffers every night, plagued with nightmares like we were. Amy and Palmer deserve no less.

Me? I still have nightmares in a way that I think I always will, but I fall back asleep right away, and I do it with my woman in my arms. With her, anything is possible. I can and will be the man that she inspires me to be. I'm going to continue to get help and work on me, but maybe this time not from a murdering psychopath.

"Dada," he says, patting my cheek with his tiny baby palms. Okay, it's more like slapping, but I'm so overcome with emotion, not just because of what today is, but because of this moment with my son—not of my body but of my heart.

"That's right, buddy. I'm your dad."

"Dada."

"Looks like he got Emma's smarts," Wes jokes, clapping me on the back and smiling at Ben.

The music changes to "The Bones" by Marren Morris and Hozier. My niece, Brooklyn, walks down the aisle holding her little brother Seth's hand and Wes's son on her hip. When she reaches the top of the aisle, Wes reaches for his boy, who happily jumps to his daddy. I love that this is the family we've built. I never would have thought even two years ago, that this is where we would all be together.

Seth joins us on the guy side while Brooklyn goes to stand over on Emma's side. I love these two, and having them in our lives is so special. I wish we could have had the opportunity to know their mother, Bonnie. And as happy as this day is, I wish their older brother, Eric, was here to share it with us and not in an undisclosed location with the U.S. Army. I wish I had held him in my arms as a baby and not met him man to man, but he's a great human being, and I am not only so proud of him, but also just so glad to know him.

"Dada," Ben babbles again, distracting me, so imagine my surprise when I see Eric walking down the aisle toward us with Claire on his arm. She has her daughter Anna on her hip. My baby sister and our oldest nephew, here for Emma and me. My heart feels like it could burst in my chest.

"What's this?" I ask when he gets to me and pulls me and Ben into a man-hug.

"I had to come meet my new cousin Benny," he says, offering Ben a high-five that ends in Eric picking up Ben's hand to pat it in his palm.

"I thought you couldn't get leave," I reply.

"It turns out my uncles have friends in high places," he says, nodding toward some seats on the edge that hold the president and his chief of staff. Both Jake and Rick served with Wes and me in the SEALs. I was shocked as shit they both not only said they would come, but they brought their wives and their secret service detail. After everything with Jane shook down, we found out every man who served on that team was a target, including Jake and Rick. And as sad as it was to find out, Ames and Palmer weren't her only victims. She had been working through the rosters for the last two years, slowly biding her time as she ingratiated herself in their lives and then struck when they least expected it.

"I'm so glad you're here."

"I wouldn't have missed it for the world," he says as he takes his place with Wes, Seth, and me.

"Dada," Ben babbles again, and I smile at him, thinking what a gift this is that he's given to me and how I could have missed it all. I could have never had him give me the word that means more than any others.

I could never have held him. One day, I'll teach him to ride a bike and throw a ball. I'll help him swim at the pool in the summers, and teach him to beat his mother and sister at bumper cars at the shore. There is a whole life ahead of us, and I almost missed it.

Thank God that was just the end of a chapter and not my whole story.

Thank God.

Everyone stands and turns, and thank fuck I'm standing at the top of the aisle, because if I weren't, I wouldn't have the most magnificent view of Emma in a strapless white dress with a full skirt that flows out around her, and at the very bottom, it looks like it was dipped in bright pink paint. Just like the ends of her hair, which are dyed the very same color and curled softly around her face like a '40s-style movie star. Instead of flowers in her arms, she carries Hope.

"Mama," Ben says, and tears pool in my eyes and flow unchecked down my cheeks.

"Yeah, buddy," I tell him. "That's your mama."

"I think maybe it's time to hand me my nephew," Eric says. "So you can greet your girl."

"Gladly," I say before handing Ben to Eric, who jumps to him happily. My boy is so lighthearted and free, and I'm glad for it.

"Hi," she says, smiling at me.

"Hi."

"Who gives this woman away?" the judge asks.

"We do," my dad says boldly. "Only my wife and I don't give her away; we welcome her with open arms."

Tears glisten in Emma's green eyes as she leans in and kisses my dad's cheek.

"I'll take this precious baby off your hands," my dad says, snatching Hope away from her mother and scurrying back to his seat by my mom, making everyone laugh.

"Dearly beloved. We are gathered here today to not only join these two people, Emma and Liam, but to unit this family," the judge says. "And usually, I would take this time to remind the couple that marriage is not for the faint of heart, that there will be good times and bad, but that in order for a strong union, love and respect must flow through those hard seasons. But Emma and Lee already know that. In fact, I've never been happier to unite two people than these two. And I married Claire and Wes last year, so that's saying something."

Everyone laughs, because we all know Wes and Claire danced around each other for years. To the point that it was painful to watch.

"Emma and Liam would like to take this time to honor those who have passed on with a moment of silence while I read their names," he says. "Mary and Robert... Anna... Bonnie... Liam.... Now, if Liam and Emma could join hands while they recite their vows." It calms me to hear that my grandparents, my sister, Anna, that they're all with us today, even if it's in spirit.

I take Emma's hands in mine and look into her eyes.

"Emma and Lee have decided to write their own vows. Emma, you begin."

"I love you, Lee," she says with a smile, even though her voice shakes with deep-felt emotion. "Today, I take you to be my husband, in good times and bad, to be my partner, my lover, and my friend. I promise to honor you and love you, even when you're wrong. I promise to be your home, your shelter in the storm, and to take you and hold you dear to me, just as you come, for the rest of my life."

"And Lee…"

"I love you, Emma. You are my home in every way, no matter where we are. I look to you, and you light the way for me in the dark. I vow to apologize when I'm wrong and not let you make me sleep on the couch more than one night when you're mad at me." She giggles and rolls her eyes. We both know that there will be no more nights of us sleeping apart for the rest of our lives. It was a major mistake that almost cost me my life. In more ways that one because Emma and the kids are my life and without them, my reason for being is gone. I had lost my way before and I can't promise that the path won't turn dark and rocky from time to time, but I'll also walk it with Emma. I've learned my lesson. "I promise to love you, to cherish you, to be a good husband and partner to you, to raise our babies by your side, and do it gratefully until the day that I die."

"Now that Emma and Liam have made their vows

to one another, let us have the rings," the judge says. "Emma, repeat after me. Lee, take this ring…"

"Lee, take this ring."

"…as a sign of my love and fidelity."

"…as a sign of my love and fidelity," she echoes.

"With it, I bestow upon you all the treasures of my mind, my heart, and my hands."

"With it, I bestow upon you all the treasures of my mind, my heart, and my hands," she finishes as she slides the solid gold band up my ring finger. "And if you ever forget that, I'll shoot you."

"Well," the judge startles. "That's an interesting addition, very non-traditional. Now, Lee, repeat after me."

I make the same vow, and I finish as I slide the solid gold band up her ring finger.

"Now, here comes the best part," the judge says. "This is the good stuff. By the power vested in me by the State of New Jersey, it is my profound pleasure that I now pronounce you husband and wife. Lee, you may kiss your bride."

I swoop Emma into my arms and crush her mouth to mine. She laughs, and I take the opportunity to lick into her mouth and deepen the kiss until catcalls and whistles remind me we're not alone… yet. But tonight, we will be. The kids are staying with my parents, and Emma and I are headed to a cabin in the Poconos.

Her cheeks blaze as bright-pink as her dress, and I

can't help but smile against her mouth. Her eyes twinkle as she looks at me and laughs. "You couldn't help yourself, could you?"

"Are you mine?" I ask, reminding her that nothing else matters. She is mine, and I am hers, and after that, it's just us and the kids. That's it. And without hesitation, she gives me the answer I need.

"Always."

"Then let's get started on our forever."

"Silly, we already have."

epic epilogue

always

Later that night

"Yes!" she pants as I drive into her from behind. I can feel the way her pussy ripples around my cock, but she's still not there yet.

"Get there," I order as I plunge into her waiting heat over and over.

"Yes."

"You're not there," I bite out as I haul her up so she's sitting on my cock.

"Nooo," she whines, but it turns into a moan when I wrap my arm like a band around her middle and pinch her nipple hard between my index finger and thumb.

I glide my other hand down the flat of her belly to

between her creamy thighs and press down on her clit. I swirl my fingers around and around her, and she tries to undulate her hips, but I'm holding her captive so she can't do anything but ride out the feeling of my hands on her body while she's impaled on my hard shaft.

"Lee," she pants. "Lee, I'm—"

"Yeah, baby," I rumble, my lips next to her ear. "You're there."

"Yes."

And then I feel her walls clamp tight over my cock, and she tosses her head back on my shoulders. Her beautiful blonde-and-pink hair fly as I hold her to me, and she comes.

Before she's done, I drop her back down to her belly on the rug in front of the fire that's blazing in the grate of our cabin, and haul her hips up so she's on her knees but the rest of her is sprawled out flat in front of me, and all of her glorious hair is tossed around.

I dig the pads of my fingers into the flesh of her hips and drive into her over and over. I plunge into her depths hard and fast and feel the walls of her pussy grip me like a tight fist around my cock.

"Yes," she moans as she comes again, and this time, I plant myself deep inside her and follow her over the edge to bliss.

When I catch my breath, I roll to the side, taking her with me. Emma curls up in my arms and snuggles in.

"Married sex is fun," she mumbles into my throat.

"Mm-hm," I mumble.

"Sex with you is always fun."

"Baby, who knew a good fucking would make you so docile." I chuckle. "I'm seeing good things for the duration of our marriage."

"Shut up," she mutters, obviously irritated.

"Who knew this was the way to keep you sweet?"

"I'm not feeling so sweet anymore, Lee."

"Then I guess I'll just have to make you that way again," I tell her as I roll her to her back and slip my fingers between her legs.

"Lee," she says as her eyes widen and flare. She digs her nails into my upper arms as she holds on, and I do not fuck around. I give her an orgasm to make her sweet again, and as she settles back into my arms once more, she closes her eyes.

"Sweet," I mumble into her hair.

"Shut up," she says.

"Are you mine?" I ask.

"Always."

Ten years later

It's crazy; that's what this is. Absolute madness. We

have three kids. Hope and Ben are both ten years old. They play soccer in the fall and baseball and softball in the spring months.

Hayley is six. She likes barbie dolls and visiting Daddy at his office and bossing around Uncle Eric and Uncle Wes. I'm almost certain she was born in a tutu, as she wears one every single day of her life, and laundry is feared by all in our household, because she raises holy hell when she has to take it off.

When she was two years old, her biological parents beat her unconscious. We took custody of her at the hospital. She occasionally has seizures, but otherwise, she seems all right. And she's smart as a fucking whip, my girl is.

We knew we were lucky that Ben had been spared any harm. For whatever reason, his biological mother stopped using drugs while she was pregnant and shielded him from that life as best as she could. Only she couldn't save herself. Hayley was not so lucky. Sometimes at night, she cries in her sleep. Hope and Ben are very protective of her. They dote on her, as do everyone who meets her. Meaning, she's spoiled, and I don't give one shit about it. She's my princess. Hope is my badass. Ben is my thoughtful deep thinker.

So this is absolutely crazy.

I pull into the driveway, having just left work minutes ago. The lights in the house are blazing, and I know homework and practice have already happened. Emma still works from home two days a week so she can be with the kids, and today was one of those days.

"Kids, dinner!" she calls when I walk through the door. "Dad is home."

I drop a kiss to her mouth, and ask, "How was your day?"

"Crazy," she says with a smile.

"Why's that?"

"Hope has a boyfriend," Ben says as he sits down at the kitchen table.

"Excuse me?" I thunder, and Hope just rolls her eyes.

"I do not," she says. "I said Jimmy Phillips threw a pencil at my head during social studies class."

"Same thing," Ben replies with a shrug, and having once been a ten-year-old boy, I can say he is not wrong.

"No, what I said is he's a moron," she adds.

She is also not wrong.

Hayley runs down the stairs at a breakneck speed and hurls her little body into my arms.

"Hey, baby girl," I greet her. "How is my princess?"

"Good," she replies. "I missed you."

"Are you sure?" I ask. "I heard Poppee took you for ice cream after school." And I know my dad did, because he texted me pictures to brag about it. He might be in his seventies, but he's a crazy old man who still gets around and does it to drive kids to sports events, or spoil them rotten.

"He did," she says, eyeing me cautiously as if I'm

about to close a trap around her.

I never thought at fifty years old I'd have a wife, two ten-year-olds, and a six-year-old, but I love every fucking minute of it. And I also never thought I'd be talking to my family about bringing home two more babies.

"So how was your day?" Emma asks as she plates up bowls of pasta and salad and passes them around the table while I pour cups of milk.

"It was good," I answer. "Interesting."

She hones in on my unsaid words. Her eyes lock on mine, and I nod, letting her know everything is okay. She unfreezes and passes another bowl.

"Actually," I say. "I have something to talk to you all about."

"What's that?" Hope asks me.

"Today, I got a phone call from my friend, Ms. Stella," I explain, and Emma gasps, because she, like me, will never forget where we met Ms. Stella. "And she told me about two little girls. Sisters."

"What about them?" Ben asks.

"Their parents hurt them really bad," I explain. "And they can't live with them anymore. And she would really like it if they could become Goodnites too."

"Well," Ben prompts softly. "Can they?"

"Here's the thing," I say. "It's not just up to me or your mom. These girls are young, one and two years old. And they've been hurt very badly."

"Like me?" Hayley whispers. We've never lied to the kids about where they came from, because while Hayley with her black hair could pass for my daughter, Ben could not. And we felt like it would dishonor his mother's sacrifices to hide the truth from him. So they all know where they came from and how they came to be Goodnites.

"Yes, baby, like you," Emma says quietly.

"Can you protect them, Daddy?" she asks me.

"I can, and I will."

"Will you be their daddy too?" she adds.

"Do you want me to be?"

"I don't know. Will I still be your princess?"

"Honey, you will be my princess even when you're eighty-five. I have no doubt about that," I answer, making Ben grin at his spaghetti.

"Then, yes," she says. "I want you to be their daddy too."

"What about you two?" I ask Hope and Ben.

"I think you know how we feel," Hope says, looking me straight in the eye. She has the Goodnite purple, and my dark hair. But she has her mama's heart and unwavering loyalty to family.

"So we're doing this?" I ask, looking at Emma.

"What are you waiting for?" Hope laughs. "Go get them!"

"I'll call Poppee," Ben says, grabbing the phone from the cradle on the kitchen counter and dialing my dad to come get them while Emma and I race around the house, grabbing her purse, my keys, and making sure the oven is off.

Ten minutes later, my mom and dad are shoving us out the front door to take our places with the kids at dinner, and Emma and I are in her new Suburban headed to the shore to meet our new daughters.

"Are we crazy?" she asks as she worries her hands in her lap.

"Probably." I laugh.

"This isn't funny, Lee. I'm getting old. You *are* old," she says.

"Hey." I grab her hand and hold it in mine on my thigh. "Are you mine?"

"Always."

"Do you want these babies?" I ask her.

"More than anything," she answers honestly.

"Then we got this."

An hour after that, we walked into the hospital and met two bruised and broken babies with brown hair, green eyes, and olive skin. And I knew instantly they were mine to love and raise and protect.

When we loaded them up in the car in the brand-new car seats we bought on the way up, just like we did when we met Ben, a calmness whispered over me. I knew it down to my bones.

My soul was happy.

My family was complete.

Eight years later

Emma sits silently, shaking beside me. She doesn't want the girls to feel her emotions. Always strong and stoic, she's struggling with today.

I put my arm around her shoulders and scoot closer to her on the metal bench of the local high school stadium to offer her some quiet comfort. Of course, this means I have to scoot my baby, Amy, over too. I can't believe she will be nine years old in two weeks. She's still my sweet, sensitive little thing that we brought home eight years ago. She likes to be with me or Ben. She's hurting today too. Parker, on the other hand, is sitting with Hayley and chatting. Where Amy belongs to the boys of the family, Parker is all girl. She adores Hayley and all things pink and ballet.

Hayley is now fourteen, and I have to give the boys in her summer driver's ed class the stink eye every day when I drop her off. Of course, it packs slightly less of a punch now that I'm fifty-eight. Whatever. I could still take them. Hayley is still bossing all of us around, still dancing, competitively now, and she's still one of the smartest people I know. Then again, all my kids are exceptional.

"And now for the graduates," the high school principal says, and Emma takes a big breath in an effort to beat back a sob.

"It'll be okay," I whisper.

"Uh huh," she says shakily while they name off the A through Fs and kid after kid make their way across the stage to accept their diplomas.

"Benjamin Liam Goodnite," they call out as Ben walks across the stage and shakes the principal's hand. We all jump to our feet, Emma and me, the girls, Claire and Wes and their brood, Eric and his family, Brooklyn and the asshole she's married to, Seth and his girlfriend, and my parents.

"Hope Ann Goodnite." Hope makes her way across the stage and accepts her diploma. Both are National Honor Society members; both excelled at sports. And where Hope is headed to college, Ben is headed to the Naval Academy. Which is what has Emma so bent out of shape. She's not mad; she's a scared mama, even though she's as proud as can be. He says he wants to be a SEAL like Wes and me. When he told me that, I had to take a moment out back to check on the sprinklers. Or at least that's what I told him. Oh, I was out back all right—crying like a baby.

"And now, a message from our valedictorian, Ben Goodnite. I've had the privilege to know Ben and his sisters, and it has been an honor to have them in this school. I can't wait to have the youngest Goodnites to fill our halls."

"You best hold onto those happy thoughts, Principal Adams," Ben says when he meets her at the mic. "Because the babies are hell on wheels."

"Hey!" they say at the same time.

"He's not wrong," I mutter under my breath, making Emma laugh through her tears and Hayley smile at her shoes.

"I want to start out by telling you all what an honor it is for me to represent the graduating class this year," Ben says into the mic before taking a breath. "And I'd like to thank the three people who are responsible for seeing me to this moment."

Emma gasps, and I hold her tighter.

"My mom and dad, I love you. Thank you for believing in me; thank you for showing me what a loving home looks like and for teaching me to live my life honestly and with honor. Thank you for showing me the kind of man I want to be." Emma sobs, and a tear runs down my cheek. "And I also want to thank my birth mother. I know. You're all shocked to learn I'm adopted and that I didn't sprout from a couple of white people," he jokes, and the crowd chuckles. "My birth mother struggled with addiction, and it took her life, but for the months she carried me and then was alive, she protected me from it. It never touched me. I know what a gift that was. And then to be taken in by good, honest people, I am so fortunate. I could have used another boy in the house with all those girls though.

"But seriously, they set the bar high with their examples of how to lead good, honest lives. I know my sister Hope and I and all of this class as we move forward from today will do it with the knowledge that our generation will lead the future. This class has seen new technology developments and innovations beyond our parents' wildest imaginations, and it is only just the beginning.

"So I will leave you to go forth and claim your future, and I hope you do it with honor, courage, and kindness. The lessons my parents taught Hope and me. Thank you."

By the time he finishes, Emma is loudly sobbing. It's time for us to go claim our graduates so we can take pictures on the field and then go back to the house for a barbeque, and Emma and I have to get it together.

"Emma, honey."

"I'm just going to miss them so much," she sobs.

"Baby, they aren't going to the moon."

"They might!" she snaps.

"We'll be all right," I tell her.

"You don't know that."

"Are you mine?" I ask her.

"Always." She sighs.

"Then I do," I say, smiling at her. "Plus, you still have three more birds to kick out of our nest before we can go back to naked Saturdays."

"Gross, Dad," Hayley grumbles.

"What's naked Saturday?" Amy asks.

"Nothing, baby," I tell her before turning back to Emma. "Now, let's go claim our kids and take some awkward cry face graduation pictures that you will cherish until you die on the field."

"Oh, all right."

And that's exactly what we do.

Seven years later

"It is with esteemed honor that we retire Chief of Police Liam Goodnite from service after thirty-five years," the mayor says. "Chief Goodnite has acted honorably and bravely throughout the course of his career, and we hope he can find time to relax in his new downtime.

I never thought I would retire. I honestly thought I would die on the job at some point in time. But then I found Emma, and then along came each of the kids, and I just kept working to put a roof over everyone's head and food on the table.

And also because I loved it.

Hearing everyone say nice things about me also makes me feel itchy, like being alive at your own funeral. I don't like it. I see Emma smiling off to the side, because she knows I tried my hardest to avoid this dog and pony show, but it was no use. The mayor wanted to be the one to hand me my gold watch and send me off into retirement as a hometown hero.

And thankfully, my hero days are long since gone. It's actually been pretty quiet since Claire and Emma retired a few years ago. Those two were apparently the source of great drama and shenanigans in the department. I was not surprised to learn this.

"And now we have a surprise," he says. "If Mrs. Goodnite could come up here to help me out. Chief Goodnite does not know, so I'll let him in on a little secret. We are about to award him with the Public Safety Medal of Valor for a lifetime of bravery and commitment to public service both as a George Washington Township Police Officer and as a Navy SEAL before that."

Emma steps up to the mayor and claims the large velvet box from him before walking her sweet ass over to me.

"Don't be mad," she says.

"I'm not."

"Liar." She winks at me.

"Chief Goodnite, we hereby bestow on you this highest of honors, which you have so richly deserved," the mayor says, and Emma plucks the medal on a black ribbon and hangs it around my neck. I have to remove my cover for her to do so, and she reaches up on her toes and places a kiss to the corner of my lips before turning to stand at my side.

The mayor makes his way over to me, and says, "Thank you for your unending devotion to the people of George Washington Township. Enjoy your retirement." And then he hands me another velvet box, this one containing the gold watch that all police officers dread, because it means their job is finally done.

There's nothing left for me to do. I feel sad and mopey, and it's really ridiculous. Emma bumps her shoulder into mine as we stand there for pictures.

"It'll be okay," she says to me. "You might like retirement with me."

"You don't know that," I grumble.

"Are you mine?" she asks, surprising me.

"Always."

"Then you know I'm right."

"That I do," I say, swinging her into my arms and kissing her deeply, because even after all these years, she's still the only one for me, and I wouldn't have it any other way. "Naked Saturdays?"

"Naked Saturdays," she confirms, and I know down to my bones I'll be happy to spend the rest of my days with this woman, however they may come.

the end

For real this time.

Thank you so much for reading *Don't Say A Word*! If you loved this, get ready to meet Jake and Grace in The Senator's Secret.

Turn the page for a sneak peek.

playlist

Whatever It Takes—Imagine Dragons

The Ones that Didn't Make it Back Home—Justin Moore

Daughter—Loudon Wainwright III

To Hell & Back—Maren Morris

Drink a Beer—Luke Bryan

Do I—Luke Bryan

Stand by You—Rachel Platten

Just Got Back from Hell—Gary Allen

Cry—Faith Hill

Fall into Me—Emerson Drive

Believer—Imagine Dragons

Far Away—Nickelback

Fell on Black Days—Soundgarden

Die Young—Kesha

Fight Song—Rachel Platten

If I Die Young—The Band Perry

Love Me Anyway—Pink ft. Chris Stapleton

The Bones—Maren Morris & Hozier

PRESIDENTIAL
AFFAIR

THE
SENATOR'S
SECRET

CAMELOT HAS ITS QUEEN

PROLOGUE

Crashing Down

"**N**o. No, no, no, no, no!"

This can't be happening. My hands shake as I flip through picture after picture. How could this have happened?

I've been so careful. I have meticulously watched every move I have ever made throughout my entire life. I never drink too much or eat too much. I have never partaken in recreational pharmaceuticals or otherwise. I don't stay out late and party. And every lover I have ever had has been not only respectable but also discreet. *Hell, the last two signed Non-Disclosure Agreements.*

I just don't know how this could've even happened.

My heart is beating so fast in my chest I feel like I might be sick. Drops of sweat are trickling down from my temples and between my breasts, and my skin is flushed hot.

But anyone looking in the windows of my palatial corner office would see exactly what I want them to. This is what I show the world every day, that I am calm, cool, and collected. I keep myself poised and in control no matter what. My hair is pulled back in a perfect ballet bun on top of my head, my makeup is light and tasteful, and my suit is Chanel. I don't play around. I have worked way too hard for my career. My reputation precedes me all over town—and *this* town is an important one.

I let the stack of glossy drug store one-hour prints fall on top of the plain manila envelope they came in where it sits on top of my mahogany desk. In secret, I call it my fancy desk. It sits proud with its elegant scrollwork carved along the edges.

I didn't grow up like this. My parents are respected attorneys here in New York, but I made the family name a commodity in high-power circles, where they need me and desperately want to know me.

I recoil from the envelope as if it's a rattlesnake sitting on my desk and not the stack of worthless paper that it is. But my conscience whispers that it's not worthless. This envelope of pictures could be *very* valuable in the right—or should I say wrong—hands. There are plenty of people here in New York who would just love to get their hands on this caliber of ammunition to use against me.

This package was sent to my office by courier with

my name type-printed on the front and a note inside written in thick block letters.

I'll be in touch.

Don't say a word.

I'm sure if I took it to the police, there would be no fingerprints either. But I can't do that. If I go to the police, this will be all over town and it will ruin my reputation. And my reputation is *everything*.

The worst part: I didn't even do it.

I tap the red-painted sole of my black patent leather Louboutins on the carpet. It's the only outward sign of my distress, and I keep that shit thoroughly hidden behind my desk. Now the question is, how do I proceed? I need to figure out what to do to keep my world from crashing down and fast.

I pick up my cellphone—the latest model that hasn't even been announced yet—and slide my carefully manicured index finger up the dark glass. It scans my face and unlocks. I scroll through my contacts until I see the one I don't want to dial with every fiber of my being. I stare it down like it's a bomb ticking down every second before it explodes in my face—just like I know this decision will later—before I finally force myself to take a deep breath and hit the Call button.

"Hello?" a whiskey-smooth voice answers. I hate that the sound of him makes me furious and my panties wet. This is definitely an unwelcome predicament.

"I need your help," I say. The words taste like sawdust on my tongue, and acid churns in my belly.

"What an interesting turn of events," he replies, and I detest how damn happy he sounds. As if my fall from greatness is something to be celebrated. Of course, he doesn't know that my life is hanging precariously in the balance.

"Don't sound so smug," I warn my adversary. "This affects you as much as it does me."

"Like I said—*interesting*. Meet me at the Magic Boarding House Tavern at eight o'clock," he says. "I'll be waiting."

I open my mouth to issue a witty putdown, but I'm too late. A dial sound goes off in my ear, letting me know that slimeball hung up on me.

My only hope now is that he can get me out of this mess. I know it's going to cost me; I just hope it's a price I'm able to pay for in one way or another. And also that I can stay strong and resist a certain U.S. senator with less than questionable morals and his stupid dimples, because sex and blackmail certainly don't mix.

Out Now!

about jennifer

Jennifer is a thirty something lover of words, all words: the written, the spoken, the sung (even poorly), the sweet, the funny, and even the four letter variety. She is a native of San Diego, California where she grew up reading the Brownings and Rebecca with her mother and Clifford and the Dog who Glowed in the Dark with her dad, much to her mother's dismay.

Jennifer is a graduate of California State University San Marcos where she studied Criminology and Justice Studies. She is also a member of Alpha Xi Delta.

14 years ago, she was swept off her feet by her very own sailor. Today, they are happily married and the parents of an 11 year old and 9 year old twins. She lives in East Texas where she can often be found on the soccer or baseball fields, drawing with her children, reading, or wondering what the hell her senior citizens have gotten up to now. Jennifer is convinced that if she puts her fitbit on one of the dogs, she might finally make her step goals.

She loves a great romance, an alpha hero, and lots and lots of laughter.

stalk her

(She Loves that Shit)

www.JenniferRebeccaAuthor.com

www.facebook.com/JenniferRebeccaAuthor

www.facebook.com/groups/JRdangerousdames

www.instagram.com/JenniferRebeccaAuthor

www.twitter.com/JenniRLreads

also by jennifer

Liam Goodnite
Hush Little Baby
Don't Say a Word

Claire Goodnite
Tell Me a Story
Tuck Me in Tight
Say a Sweet Prayer
Kiss Me Goodnight

A Presidential Affair
The Senator's Secret
Caught by the Chief of Staff
The Press Secretary's Passion

Royal Secrets and Lies
King of Lies
Crown of Thorns
Save the Queen

Funerals and Obituaries
I Met a Girl
Dead and Buried
Dead and Gone
Dead and Deceived
Dead and Wed, TBD

Murder on Ice
Attack Zone
Layback

Southern Heartbeats
Stand
Joy
Whiskey Lullaby
Mercy
Just a Dream, TBD
If Tomorrow Never Comes
Church Bells, TBD

Standalones
Trap: A Salvation Society Novel, TBD
Dark Horse: A Driven World Novel, TBD

For a complete updated list, visit:

www.jenniferrebeccaauthor.com/books

acknowledgements

Thank you thank you thank you for reading Don't Say a Word and for loving the Goodnite siblings as much as I do. I hate to see them go, but who knows, maybe one day the kids will lead a whole new generation of Goodnites on adventures. I know that this was a hard one to get through. It was for me too. So very much so. Thank you for giving it a chance.

Thank you to Tricia Crouch for sticking by me on this ride. I would be lost without her.

Thank you to Alyssa Garcia for everything. For keeping me on track, for helping me see the bigger picture and promising me wine at the end. I am so glad that this journey is ours to share. Bottoms up, bish. Don't ever leave me.

Thank you to Kayla Robichaux for making me sound so good, for cheering me on and being an all around awesome human being. I'm so glad to know you. You knocked this out of the park and I owe you big time! Don't ever leave me either.

Thank you to my personal cheerleaders: Alyssa, Stacy, Emma, Ann, Jessica, and Andrea. For knowing how hard this book was for me to write and pushing me to get through it. I needed to do it and you knew it. Thank you.

Thank you to my parents for loving me, for supporting me through the dark moments and sticking by me. I owe everything to you.

Thank you to my husband, Sean. I thank God every day that you walked into that apartment and noticed me. For whatever put you in my path. Thank you for standing by me and supporting me, for loving me whether I deserve it or not. You're the real deal, my hero, my heart, my everything. It was always you.